BILBAO–
NEW YORK–
BILBAO

BILBAO–
NEW YORK–
BILBAO

Kirmen Uribe

Translated from the Basque
by Elizabeth Macklin

SPATIAL SPECIES SERIES

Youmna Chlala and Ken Chen, series editors

COFFEE HOUSE PRESS

Minneapolis
2022

First U.S. edition published 2022
Copyright © 2008 by Kirmen Uribe
Translation © 2014 by Elizabeth Macklin
Foreword © 2022 by Youmna Chlala
Cover art and design by Mika Albornoz
Book design by Mika Albornoz
Author and translator photographs © 2022 by Richard Rothman

Coffee House Press books are available to the trade through our primary distributor, Consortium Book Sales & Distribution, cbsd.com or (800) 283-3572. For personal orders, catalogs, or other information, write to info@coffeehousepress.org.

Coffee House Press is a nonprofit literary publishing house. Support from private foundations, corporate giving programs, government programs, and generous individuals helps make the publication of our books possible. We gratefully acknowledge their support in detail in the back of this book.

LIBRARY OF CONGRESS CATALOGING-IN-PUBLICATION DATA

Names: Uribe Urbieta, Kirmen, 1970– author. | Macklin, Elizabeth, translator.
Title: Bilbao-New York-Bilbao / Kirmen Uribe ; translated from the Basque by Elizabeth Macklin.
Other titles: Bilbao-New York-Bilbao. English
Description: First U.S. edition. | Minneapolis : Coffee House Press, 2022. | Series: Spatial species series
Identifiers: LCCN 2021056945 | ISBN 9781566896498 (paperback)
Subjects: LCSH: Bilbao (Spain)—Fiction. | New York (N.Y.)—Fiction. | LCGFT: Novels.
Classification: LCC PH5339.U55 B5513 2022 | DDC 899/.923—dc23/eng/20220420
LC record available at https://lccn.loc.gov/2021056945

Printed in the United States of America

29 28 27 26 25 24 23 22   1 2 3 4 5 6 7 8

Say the most personal thing, say it, nothing else
matters. Don't be ashamed. The generalities
can be found in the newspaper.

Elias Canetti

Since then I've wondered which are in fact those
invisible relationships that define our own life,
and what thread ties them all together.

W. G. Sebald

But once they drop anchor, once the cranes
begin their dipping and their swinging,
it seems as if all romance were over.

Virginia Woolf

CONTENTS

FOREWORD

Dear Kirmen,

While reading your novel, I floated in its suspended narratives, hanging above and below the sea. Poems, emails, and letters. Ekphrasis as a method of reassembling a place. A family history on the precipice of disappearing or perhaps simply regenerating. And the Basque Country, a place on the edge of the sea and the nation-state.

Simultaneously, your narrator is writing his own book, a fictional, uncompleted novel that becomes a space for the reader to also invent. The narrator seems to seek a feeling of optimism, a light, something to believe in that exists only in this yet-to-be-written novel. In his search, he discovers familial and communal stories cut too short. You describe the book's structure as a net, an algorithm, and we sense the narrator knotting together these histories into a fraught yet constructed whole.

As readers, we follow, accelerate, remember, rewind, speculate. We sit next to your narrator on a plane, a boat, in a museum, on the shore, or near the fragile windows of his bedroom. A window can be transparent or reflective, like the sky and sea that act as "double-dyed blue" mirrors in the book. They refract truths and fictions. You write in a prismatic line that distorts the symmetry between sea and sky, grandfather and grandchild, map and boat, climate and hunger, language and desire, city and city, and move it closer to what I imagine as the complex ecosystem where sea and land meet.

Your narrator proposes that the Basque "literary tradition bears a resemblance to Agirre's parents' house, small, poor, disorderly." But the worst thing is its being secret. He says, "We need to invite the people passing by to come into our house and offer them something there, even if that something is hardly anything." Then he reminds us that "the best way to air out a house is to open up the windows."

The book has so many open windows that the crosscurrents blow us from one corner of the house to another. What does it mean to let someone in? What are the risks and mistranslations and how do they become openings and transformations? While reading your book, I could not help but feel the joy of possibilities and discovery, the way that despite everything, fish reveal their age once they are cut open. If you know how to read them, they tell you what they have been through. But first, there's the cut, the severing that is exile.

Youmna Chlala, series editor

BILBAO–
NEW YORK–
BILBAO

1

BILBAO

Fish and trees are alike.

They're alike because of the growth rings. Trees have these in their trunks. Cut through a tree trunk and there will be the rings. A year for each ring, and that's how you know what the tree's age is. Fish have them, too, but in their scales. And just as we do with trees, we know by those growth rings what the animal's age is.

Fish are always growing. Not us, we start shrinking once we've reached maturity. Our growth stops and our bones begin to knit together. A person shrivels. Fish, though, grow until they die. Faster when they're young, and as the years go by more slowly, but fish always go on growing.

Winter creates the growth rings of a fish. It's the time when fish eat least, and that time of hunger draws a dark trace in the fish scale. In that winter season when the fish grows least. Not in summer, though. When there's no hunger there's no trace at all left behind in the fish scale.

The growth ring of a fish is microscopic, you can't see it with the naked eye, but there it is. As if it were a wound. A wound that hasn't healed up.

1

And, as with the growth rings of fishes, terrible events stay on in our memory, mark our life, until they become a measure of time. Happy days go fast, on the other hand – too fast – and we forget them quickly.

What winter is for fish, loss is for humans. Loss makes our time specific for us, the end of a relationship, the death of a person we love.

Each loss a dark growth ring deep down.

The day they told him he had a scant few months left to live, our grandfather didn't want to go home. Our mother, his young daughter-in-law, accompanied him to the doctor's office that morning. Granddad listened calmly to what the doctor was saying. He heard him out without a peep and, afterward, shook his hand and courteously said goodbye.

When they left the consulting room, Mum didn't know what to say. After a long silence, she asked him if they'd be heading along to the bus to Ondarroa now. He said no.

"We're not going back yet. We'll spend the day in Bilbao. I want to show you something," he said to her, and made an effort to smile.

Granddad took Mum to the Bilbao Fine Arts Museum. She would never forget that day, how on the very day they told him he was going to die Granddad took her to a museum.

How he attempted to place beauty above death, without success. How he attempted to make that terrible day have another kind of memory for her. Our mother would always remember that gesture of his.

That was the first time she'd ever set foot in a museum.

Forty-five years later I went to the same museum myself. I wanted to find out about a certain picture, and so I went. I was on the trail of a picture by the painter Aurelio Arteta, as if following a half-erased clue, in some totally intuitive way. An inner voice kept telling me that that picture was important, that it would turn out to be an essential piece in the novel that I was writing.

The picture is a mural, painted, as it happens, in the Ondarroa country house the architect Ricardo Bastida had built to spend summers in. It was in the summer of 1922 that Arteta painted the mural, there in the living room. In the nineteen-sixties, though, a few years after Ricardo Bastida died, his family sold the house. The buyers razed it to build apartments. But the mural was saved, by good luck. Aurelio Arteta's artwork was taken down and to the museum in Bilbao. It's been on exhibit ever since, in one of the upstairs galleries.

Jose Julian Bakedano, one of the museum's curators, showed it to me. In its day the mural took up three walls of the Bastidas' living room. In the museum, though, it's hung on one wall as a triptych. In the very center is the representation of an outing to a country fair, that's the largest of the pieces. And on the outer wings come the two other pictures. One is of a woman of the era, posed just like a Renaissance Venus. The other is of a young couple, talking with each other in the shade of a tree.

At first sight, the mural's colours are the surprising thing about it. Arteta uses very bright colours to portray the boys and girls on their way to the fair: greens, blues, lilacs. And in a way that had never been done before.

"At the outset, a number of critics didn't have much regard for Arteta's work," Bakedano told me. "Mocking him, they said he wore coloured spectacles to paint in. The years he spent studying painting in Paris were plain as day in Arteta's work. He took a house in Montmartre and there he fell in love with the work of Toulouse-Lautrec and Cézanne. But he never wanted to make a complete break with tradition. It's precisely because of this, I think, that his pictures put me in mind of an old tavern that's been painted in bright colours – they're modern but without losing their charm."

In the mural two worlds appear, together at one and the same time. On one side are the *baserritarrak,* the people of the farmsteads, and on the other the townsfolk. The farm girls are in traditional dress. Their skirts come down to their ankles, scarves on heads and their necklines modest. The city girls, though, don't look like that at all. Their dresses are lightweight, the wind moves them. Their hemlines are shorter, their knees allowed to show, and their necklines are wide open. What's more, on their breasts they sport jewelry. Compared with the *baserritarrak,* the city girls look beckoning, as if they were courting the onlooker. The Art Deco effect is as clear as can be here, that nineteen-twenties optimism wells from these paintings.

"This picture represents the leap from old world to new," Bakedano explained now, "and the contrast between farm folk and city folk intensifies the city girls' eroticism."

The Bastida-house mural was actually just a rehearsal. Aurelio Arteta had not yet mastered mural technique and the architect let him use his living room to try things out. The real work would come a bit later. Ricardo Bastida himself designed the headquarters the Bank of Bilbao was going to have in Madrid. In its day, that building, to be built right on the Calle de Alcalá, would be unique. Of necessity it would be a symbol of the bank and, more broadly, of the city of Bilbao. A gesture of power and modernity. The work would make the careers of both Bastida and Arteta, and win them recognition outside the Basque Country.

Bastida wanted Aurelio Arteta to be the artist for the bank's great hall. The two of them had known each other ever since they were children, and their lives were strikingly alike, one in architecture, the other in painting. For the rotunda of the bank's entrance hall Arteta would paint an allegory of Bilbao. The stevedores, the workers from the steel mills of the era, the *baserritarrak*, the fishmongers and more. It was a taxing job, more than ten murals, and moreover on an irregular surface.

Arteta took the commission but wanted to get himself well prepared beforehand. He was exacting, it was hard for him to consider a work finished. Once, years later, during his exile in Mexico, a prospective buyer attempted to look at an unfinished canvas that was hidden under a cloth, lifting the covering. When Arteta saw him at it, he took up his palette knife in a rage and slashed the man's face. It was the one thing said to drive him wild.

A perfectionist to a fault, Arteta took great pains with every detail. He didn't care much about signing his paintings, often enough left them with his name off, as if he couldn't be bothered. With money matters, too, he was sloppy. Nevertheless, while he was painting he went at it body and soul. And, even to paint the mural in Ondarroa, he had the water brought in from Madrid, so that when it came time to start work in Madrid the water would be sure to have the same density. He chose the best materials. The sand would be ground from genuine Markina marble.

I had heard a lot of things about Arteta, and also about his character. He was a beloved painter in his lifetime. He was well regarded by conservatives, nationalists, and socialists alike. "His bashful nature may have influenced that," Bakedano added.

I'd also heard about how he fled to Mexico during the civil war. After the aerial bombing of Guernica, Spain's legitimate government commissioned Arteta to paint a meaningful picture for the Paris Exposition. The whole world would know then what had happened in Guernica, what kind of massacre the Nazis had committed there. It would have been his life's great work. Arteta refused the commission, however. He explained that he was sick of the war, he would prefer to join his family in exile in Mexico. The commission later fell to Pablo Picasso. And we all know what comes after that. Doing the Guernica picture would have been a huge advance in Arteta's career, but he turned it down. He chose life over art. He preferred being with his family to being remembered in the future.

Many people will see Arteta's choice as an error. However could he miss out on his chance of a lifetime because of a fleeting emotional reaction. How had he placed the people he loved above his art. There will be those, too, who will never forgive him for it, in the belief that a creator's obligation is to their creative gift above all else.

More than once I've wondered what I'd do if I were in Arteta's predicament. Which way I'd choose.

You can't tell, you have to live through the same situation to do so. But it's the very crossroads an artist often ends up facing. Personal life or creation. Arteta obviously took the first route, and Picasso the second.

Jose Julian Bakedano went off to his office and back to work, but before he did he gave me the documentation the museum had on the Arteta mural: how their conservators effected its removal from Bastida's house.

In any event, he gave me a piece of advice. "The person who knows the most about the mural is Carmen Bastida, the architect's daughter, the best thing would be to call her," and he handed me her phone number on a Post-it, saying, "Tell her you're calling her because I said to," and went back to his work.

I stayed behind on my own, staring at the mural, thinking. The optimism that emanated from it attracted me most of all. That energy made by the brushstrokes of Arteta's hand. Back in that summer of 1922 Arteta and Bastida had great hopes for their work, they had no fear of the future. That strength dazzled me. Not knowing what would happen to them in just a few years' time.

—

About my grandfather I don't know too much. Liborio Uribe. By the time I was born he was dead and our father didn't talk to us a lot about his father. He wasn't big on the past, himself. A seaman by nature, he preferred to look to the future. About the people in our mother's family, on the contrary, yes: we know a thousand tales from Mum's side, stories about one relation and another. But on our dad's side very few. Maybe because of this, that grandfather made me curious.

Among the few things our father did tell was a memory from his childhood, about the way of life in the summertimes. I'd heard him say how when he was little he'd be on the beach the whole day, at the wooden changing rooms Granddad kept for the summer people. He'd help his parents with any number of chores: taking basins of water to the summer people, helping them rinse off, getting the sand off their legs and hanging their bathing clothes on the drying poles. I imagine him entirely silent at this work, carrying water and picking up clothing and, between times, paying attention to the things the summer people said to each other.

"I remember your father very well, he was a graceful boy and a worker," Carmen Bastida said to me when I paid her a visit at her house in Bilbao. "Those were the best years of my life. Life held no worries for me then, no adversity."

The Bastida family had three bathing cabanas on the beach. They used to set them up high on the sand, close to the cliffs. Next door was the stretch of beach for the people who engaged in therapeutic nudism, shielded by a tall length of dark cloth. The beach days come gathered together in black-and-white photographs. Showing me the photographs, Carmen tried to explain who each person was. To go by what Bastida's daughter said, painters, musicians, architects, astronomers met up on the beach at the Bastidas' cabanas. Most of them coming from Bilbao and Madrid. "But what I loved best was a man from the town, Liborio, the stories he used to tell us."

Keeping the cabanas was not Granddad's only way of making a living. He had a small boat, too, to take out fishing, by the name of *Dos Amigos.* The name of the boat always made me wonder: *Dos Amigos* – Two Friends. Why ever had he named his boat that, how had he come up with that weird name. And if Granddad himself had been one of the two friends, who had the other one been.

I wanted to unearth that other one, discover why all trace of him had been wiped out. Whether Granddad had gotten angry at his friend. Wanting to answer those questions, several years ago I started tracking down the clues. I felt that *Dos Amigos* had a novel somewhere inside it, a novel about the fishing world that's in the process of disappearing.

But this was the plan only at the outset. And the search for facts for the novel has taken me down several roads I hadn't expected, I've met up with many surprises.

To find out fishes' age you need to count the growth rings on the scales, and add one year. When they're larvae, fish don't have any scales. In the case of eels, you have to add four years. Since eels spend four years as larvae.

They likewise need four years to cross the Atlantic. The tiny elvers make the trip from the Sargasso Sea to the Bay of Biscay in that much time.

My plane will cover the same distance in seven hours. I'll be taking a flight to New York on this very day, from the Bilbao airport.

2

A COFFEE AT THE AIRPORT

I get to the airport from Ondarroa before I thought I would. The sky over Bilbao a double-dyed blue. Even though it's November it's clear the south wind is going to be warming up the countryside. Autumn is our season for the south wind. In this autumn of 2008, I turned thirty-eight. This autumn when Obama's just beat out McCain in the presidential race. I have to get on a flight from Bilbao to Frankfurt and from there to New York.

When I go to the Lufthansa counter to check in I hear a ruckus nearby, a surprise, the Athletic Club soccer players were right there, about to get on a plane. And with them the cameras and the press. The players answer their questions with optimism. With a make-believe optimism. An optimism nobody believes in.

Optimism can even hurt you.

Once I've checked my bag I get away as soon as possible, to the airport café. Noontime light had taken over the café. Sunbeams streamed in through the tall plate-glass windows. You could see golden flecks in the air, golden light, in the café with its floor awash in paper napkins and its tables full up with dirty dishes.

A boy ordering at the bar starts talking to me.

"What it's like to be famous," he says. "The TV and the rest of them all show up to send off the players. They'll never do that sort of sendoff for our dad. He's heading out to Chile for six months, to fish. He does six months at sea and two months home."

A fisherman, and he ships out without a boat, by airplane. It strikes me that the airport's become the quay of an earlier era.

"Our dad was a fisherman too," I tell him. "He worked the seas up north, on the grounds they call Rockall."

The boy's face stabilises.

"It could be he might know our dad, then . . . ," he says to me, before he takes up his glasses and makes for their table.

This is what Wikipedia has to say about Rockall island in its entry:

Rockall

Rockall is a small, rocky islet in the North Atlantic. The rock is part of an extinct volcano and is located at 57°35′48″N 13°41′19″W. It lies 301.4 kilometres west of the uninhabited islands of St. Kilda, Scotland, and 368.7 kilometres west of the crofting township of Hogha Gearraidh, on the island of North Uist.

It is 424 kilometres northwest of Donegal in the Republic of Ireland. Rockall is about 25 metres wide at its base and rises to a height of 22 metres above sea level. The rock's only permanent inhabitants are periwinkles and other mollusks. Small numbers of seabirds, among them kittiwakes, guillemots and gannets, use the rock to rest on in summer. It is impossible to live there. It has no natural source of fresh water.

"It's impossible to live here," Maria Gabina Badiola, our great-grandmother on Dad's side, apparently thought, about Ondarroa. That's what I gathered especially from our father's aunt Maritxu in Bilbao, the youngest of our grandmother Ana's sisters.

When I took up the project of the novel for the umpteenth time, in the spring of 2005, Maritxu was the first person I interviewed. She was the only family member still living from Liborio and Ana's generation. Our grandparents were dead on both Dad's side and Mum's.

When I paid her a visit I heard stories I'd never, ever heard before, ones Dad never told us. The exact names and dates get fuzzy, but I realised that our dad's whole family history was made up of round trips, flights and returnings.

And always in the background that connection to the sea, oftenest tragic, comical as a matter of course.

Maritxu lives in Bilbao, in the Begoña neighbourhood. Maria Gabina Badiola, her mother, when she was widowed, gathered up her children and made for Bilbao, she wanted nothing more to do with the seafaring life. They'd brought her husband home dead from the sea, and her father had drowned as well. They'd seen from the town watchtower how the catboat *San Marcos* went down right there in the bay, and how it was that Maria's father, Canuto Badiola, had drowned, along with her brother, Ignacio. They didn't find Canuto's body.

So close and unable to do a thing. A few years later Arteta would paint a similar scene, in the canvas called "The Northwester."

To Bilbao they all went with their mother and turned their backs on the sea. Great-grandmother Maria and every one of the children started work at the Echevarría smeltery, "making nails and horseshoes, nails and horseshoes by the thousands."

Maritxu told me stories I didn't know. One about two brothers from Mutriku, for instance, who went to Argentina to work. One of the brothers was blinded in an accident and wanted to go back to the town they'd been born in. His brother helped him on the voyage home. Boarding a ship in

Buenos Aires, they crossed the Atlantic and to get to their village boarded a train. They got as far as Deba. The train station was four kilometres away from their town. Leaving his blind brother at the depot, the other brother simply went off, back to Argentina. After an odyssey of thousands of kilometres, he reboarded the train to cross the ocean again. With his birthplace a mere four kilometres distant, he didn't want to see his home. He left his brother sitting right there all alone. Some nuns finally took charge of the blind man and they brought him home.

Maritxu spoke in Ondarroan, our town's Basque dialect, but as it had been spoken eighty years before. Periodically she'd drop into Spanish, a legacy of the years she'd lived in Bilbao.

And she also told me how the sister of those two brothers, Josefa Ramona Epelde, married the carpenter Isidro Odriozola. The carpenter must have been an elegant man, one of those men who wore gleaming-white suits. He was from Azpeitia, in the neighbouring province, and came to work in the Ondarroa boatyards. But to find himself a wife he went to Mutriku. He didn't want any Biscayan females and so he crossed the border between the two provinces, to marry in Mutriku.

When their son Jose Francisco got married, Isidro built all of their furniture out of scraps of boats. In Ondarroa people called Jose Francisco Odriozola "Tubal." The man who would be Maritxu and Grandmother Ana's father. He had the nickname "Tubal" because he had a boat of that name. From what Maritxu said, Great-grandfather called the vessel Tubal after a book he liked. He read from it every single night.

Tubal, according to the Bible, was a grandson of Noah, and he ended up by chance at the Tower of Babel. Esteban Garibai's volume *Los cuarenta libros del compendio historial de las chronicas y universal historia de todos los reynos de España* explains that one of the 72 languages created at the Tower of Babel was Basque, and that it was in precisely that language that Tubal suddenly began to speak. Yes indeed, in Basque. He came to the Iberian Peninsula and settled in comfortably there. This took place 142 years after the Great Flood, in 2163 B.C., all the while relying on the accounts in that old volume.

Tubal Odriozola was a hard-working man. He made a deal with a businessman from Navarre named Otxagabia to build his boat. A deal of a certain era, a spoken agreement, nothing written down on paper. Otxagabia would put in the money and Tubal the labour. The boat would belong to both of them, but one would remain ashore and the other would work at sea, as captain. And that's how he'd pay off his debt.

Tubal made good, and even made strides in politics. In Ondarroa they put him in charge of the San Pedro harbor association. He made friends in Bilbao. It was just around that very time that he met the head of the Echevarría plant.

For Maritxu those were the happiest years. At home they lacked for nothing. Tubal's last years were hard, though, Otxagabia didn't carry out their spoken agreement and Tubal was left without a boat. He made dozens of trips to the courthouse in Burgos in hopes of a decision in his favor. To no avail. He was obliged to work as crew during his final years. Having come down with a mouth infection, he was brought home from sea dead.

Maritxu recalls very well the last time she saw her father. From a distance he was looking out for his little girl. He signalled with his hands, laying one on top of the other in a stroking caress. Maritxu made the same gesture to me, two hands caressing. It means "Love you, love you," my aunt explained in her diction of eighty years ago.

I hadn't known of that hand sign, it must have been a signal lost long before.

Maritxu didn't tell me much at all about Grandmother Ana. Maritxu's sister was a worker, and that was what killed her, her body sickened out of pure exhaustion. "She should have stayed in Bilbao and not gone back to the village." But Ana fell in love with a fisherman named Liborio and married in Ondarroa, leaving her mother and her brothers and sisters in Bilbao.

"Your grandmother went through a lot. During the war, too, she was alone for a year, without her husband. She took an official from Franco's side into her home, Javier, and also a lady whose mother was a prisoner in the women's prison at Saturraran."

I frowned.

"Yes, I know it's startling to have people from both sides in your home in wartime. But ideas are one thing and the heart is another."

Ideas are one thing and the heart is another. I remember Maritxu's words when my flight is called. I pass the table where the fisherman who's on his way to Chile sits with his family. They're sitting in silence. They don't say a word to me. At the security checkpoint I put my computer bag, jacket, and belt on the conveyor and go through the little portal. It doesn't emit a sound.

I pick up my things, and look back. People standing in line to go through security. I don't see anyone I know. I think of Maritxu's hand sign. The gesture her father made to her that last time. It was a signal between the two of them, a secret between the two of them. The final one.

And I feel like making the same sign to somebody from a distance: laying one hand on top of the other in a caress, saying, "Love you, love you," silently.

3

TREASURES IN HIDING

I went to New York for the first time in March of 2003, at just about the same time the ultimatum President Bush gave the Iraqis was about to expire. I went with a few musician friends, invited by Elizabeth, who had translated some of my poems, to do some performances at a few places in Manhattan. At one of them, a space called the Bowery Poetry Club, a New York writer named Phillis Levin told me the most glorious definition I'd ever heard on the subject of languages.

She'd found the Basque language fascinating, she told me. She'd heard of our language before then, too, had come across texts written in Basque. On the Internet and elsewhere. More than once she'd tried to guess at what those words might mean. Hadn't even come close. But something had caught her eye: all the x's that appeared in the texts.

"Your language looks like a treasure map," she said, "if you just forget all the rest of the letters and focus in on the x, it looks as if you could find out where the treasure is."

I thought it was the most glorious thing you could say of a language you didn't know, that it's the map to a treasure.

—

A lost treasure was what the Impressionist painter Darío de Regoyos was searching for his whole life long. The revolution of Impressionism was: they didn't want to paint the way people were teaching them to paint in the academies. Up until then people did in fact learn how to paint a horse, but they weren't looking at real horses. All they had to do was follow cast models. Learn the technical tricks. And so, the Impressionists decided to leave the academies behind and go outdoors. To paint what they saw with their own eyes. It was to paint landscapes of their very own that the first of them came to the Cantabrian coast. The seaside light was what they wanted to capture on these canvases of theirs.

Darío de Regoyos spent Holy Week of 1906 in Ondarroa. It wasn't his first time. He'd often come here to paint. He mostly painted seascapes, coastal vistas, the fishing vessels going out at dawn's first light, or when they came back in, in the afternoon.

He took a room in the elegant Hotel de la Bahía along with his wife. Those were reportedly happy times in the Regoyoses' life. The painter felt strong and optimistic. And one sign of that strength is the work he did during those days. In three or four days he painted the canvas called "The Departure of the Tuna Boats." Almost at one go. And what's more, he ended up happy with the work. He was proud of that picture and even said so to friends, that that very picture was perhaps his best. Regoyos was so proud of the picture that thoughout his lifetime he never wanted to sell it, and he carried it with him on his travels, perhaps as a memento of those happy days.

When he died, a businessman named Gregorio Ibarra bought it. Unfortunately, the picture was subsequently lost in the 1936 war. Since then no one's ever managed to unearth a trace of it. A mystery grew up around it, where could the picture be, had it been destroyed or had it ended up in some forgotten corner. As the mystery increased, the picture's renown increased as well.

"It was a picture of immense melancholy; the broad sea beneath a tragic and gleaming ruddy sky" – so the critic Rodrigo Soriano described it. "And far out the boats' great sails, as if they were gigantic yellow banners, there above the water in which they falteringly make their endless procession." Another critic of the time, Juan de la Encina, attempted a sketch of the picture. But there all trace of the painting is lost.

More than once I've told myself it might not be bad to write a thriller about the intrigue surrounding the painting. But actually, another mystery was keeping me up at night. If it was Holy Week, how could he have been painting tuna boats? You don't catch tuna till after St. Peter's Day, after all, and that's at the end of June! Was the man mixed up about this, or had he really, truly spent such happy days, so happy as to make for that kind of careless error?

After Darío de Regoyos a lot of painters came in questing after the coastal light. That was until the civil war began. Their favorite scene was the old bridge. The brothers Zubiaurre and Adolfo Guiard, and Aurelio Arteta himself, set down on canvas the contours of the medieval bridge that crosses the Artibai River in Ondarroa.

Aurelio Arteta began coming to Ondarroa to paint in the nineteen-tens. He apprenticed himself to the Zubiaurre brothers there. He painted the bridge the way they had. Still, Arteta was longing for something more modern, to take a step forward. For him the bridge wasn't a symbol of lost golden ages. If the bridge was the symbol of Basqueness, as some people had said, he would give it a different look.

As early as 1910 Arteta made the painting now known as "The Bridge." In it a steamboat is crossing under the bridge. He put the steamer in on purpose, so as to contrast it with the bridge's medieval air. That isn't the only innovation either. He used a technique from photography in painting the picture, and it strongly resembles the illustrations that contemporary painters had started doing for the newspapers.

Among the paintings of the era is another one that surprises me. "Sending Off the Launches." In it four women are bidding goodbye to the boats going off to sea. One of them holds a child in her upraised hands. Come back one way or another, she wants to tell her husband, his baby is right there waiting for him.

Just this past July I saw a photograph on the Internet. It showed a wooden skiff on its way to the Canary Islands. They'd spent days and days adrift at sea, and at long last a rescue boat was about to rescue them. The women held up their children so they'd be seen from the rescue boat, so they'd know there were children aboard. The image of those African women was Arteta's very image.

One of Arteta's models was Benigna Burgoa. Benigna was a lithe eighteen-year-old at the time. Arteta saw her on the street and asked if she'd pose for him. She went home all happy and told her parents of the conversation she'd had with the painter, but they gave her a scolding.

Modelling was something fallen women did, they told her, and don't even think of it. Since they knew Benigna had been happy around the painter, they forbade her to leave the house. She could go only as far as the old bridge, to the fountain by the bridge, for water. But since Benigna was a live wire, and knew there was usually a long line at the fountain for water, she arranged to leave her water jug with an acquaintance and, with that pretext, go on to Arteta's studio to do some modelling. So that's how Arteta painted her portraits, in those fountain intervals.

And Benigna kept her secret so well that no one knew a thing until many, many years had gone by. Benigna was already dead when, once, for a celebration in the old quarter, they put up reproductions of Arteta's pictures in the shop-windows, along with old photographs. At a single glance at one of the pictures, "That's Grandma Benigna," one of her grandchildren said. And so it happened that they learned that their grandmother had had a bad reputation and failed to mind what her parents told her.

Being a model was not at all easy in a certain era. It became even harder during the Franco years, from what another painter, Felix Beristain, told me.

Beristain had met the Zubiaurre brothers, the painters. They had their studio on North Street, because the light came in from the north there, and north light, which throws the fewest shadows, is the best to paint by. The Zubiaurres managed to get Beristain a grant during the Franco times. Two hundred seminarians got all the rest of the grants and they gave only one for painting, and that one went to Beristain.

One way or another the Zubiaurres even found him a small studio in Ondarroa, beneath the church bell tower. The place was the equivalent of the municipal glory hole, and the young artist had to make do amidst the ancient rubbish to do his painting: old flags, the papier-mâché Carnaval big-heads, brooms and whatnot.

The banned books were also stored in that same attic. We're in luck, he said to himself, thinking he'd find hidden pleasures in those books, highways to every sin. But the banned books turned out to be no big deal, they were too innocent for that. There in the pile were books by Baroja, Kipling, Stevenson.

An uncle of ours, Uncle Boni, happened to spend some time there, too, since besides being a glory hole, the studio also did service as the town jail. And because he once went out during a storm warning in spite of the ban, they sentenced him to a day or two in that old attic. He was way too fond of fishing.

So they both seemingly had a good long look at the forbidden books.

Models made their way up to the studio from time to time too. The owner of the pharmacy beside the church took note and complained to the vicar: so what kind of indecent hanky-panky were those young ladies engaged in, there in the bell tower?

In the end, they shut down Beristain's studio.

They didn't close the jail, however.

A monster, a monster that roars. In the old Irish legends Rockall island is called Rocabarraigh. The rock that roars. According to Celtic tradition, the third time the rock comes to light, it's said the end of the world will arrive. For the rock does appear and disappear. It's visible only in summer, in winter waves cover it, until they've made it disappear.

The phenomenon of extreme waves hasn't been much studied by scientists. The accounts of seamen have always been taken to be myth, when they'd say that the waves around Rockall would get to be the size of mountains. No one believed them, they were surely exaggerating.

Our father used to tell us that very thing too, the waves in winter got to be the size of our house. We lived in a seven-story apartment building, on the fifth floor. And so the waves would reach all the way to the roof, he said. And the three of us brothers and our sister would say to him, "No way," thinking he was aiming to show off.

He didn't get angry.

Among scientists, though, it was said until quite recently that the largest of waves would reach no higher than fifteen metres. Even when the seamen themselves said otherwise.

Extreme waves have nothing to do with tsunamis. Those are created by earthquakes and become extreme only once they make landfall, once they touch the seafloor. More than one fisherman has told me that tsunamis passed right under their boat without their even knowing. If you're running in high seas, they're not the least bit dangerous.

The phenomenon of extreme waves, though, is something else again. When people began making measurements by satellite they realised there are many more extreme waves in the Atlantic than was previously thought. But by the satellite measurements you couldn't really tell what the waves' height was. To tell that, you actually had to be at sea.

In February of 2000, they discovered the largest wave ever measured off the coast of northern Scotland's Rockall island. The ship RSS *Discovery* measured it on February 8th that year, between six in the evening and six in the morning. The ship's position was 57.5°N and 12.7°W, east of Rockall, two hundred and fifty kilometres from Scotland. The wind was out of the west.

A team led by the scientist Naomi P. Holliday made the discovery. The strangest thing is that such waves do not form in the largest storms. In measurements made from ships and buoys during hurricanes, those made during Hurricane Ivan for instance, 17.9-metre waves were measured at most.

In the results section of a 2006 scientific paper in Volume 33, L05613, of *Geophysical Research Letters*, "Were extreme waves in the Rockall Trough the largest ever recorded?," Naomi Holliday said this: "The significant wave height of 18.5 m is greater than any previously published wave data, and the maximum individual wave height of 29.1 m is amongst the largest. . . . Satellite altimeter data has been shown to underestimate extreme wave heights, so there is clearly a need for more direct deep ocean wave measurements by buoys and ships."

Twenty-nine point one metres. I remembered Dad's measurements. Seven-story house. Seven times three, twenty-one. Then you would have to add on the ground floor. Say that's four metres. Twenty-five. Two more for the roof. Twenty-seven metres. He was right, that wave would have covered our house.

4

16-MILLIMETRE SHORT SUBJECTS

Planes leave Bilbao on a seaward heading. Once airborne the plane follows Bilbao's estuary, toward the open sea. We take the route the freighters that used to go down the Ibaizabal River took at one time. When the south wind is up, you can see the countryside clear as clear. The old cranes along Bilbao's river, the factories, the new superport.

Where we live a south wind is the norm in the fall. If it starts in October the mild weather can hang on almost until Christmas. Our maternal grandmother, Anparo, used to say that that winter of 1936 was mild as could be, it hardly snowed at all. As if God had wanted to mellow the war, as if He'd taken pity on our fighting men. That's how she put it.

When we get to the sea, the plane banks to the right, Galea Point, the beaches at Sopelana, and just past them Urdaibai, Guernica. As soon as we reach the area around Ondarroa and Mutriku, the plane heads inland, making for the wide-open continent, on its way to Frankfurt.

Between Ondarroa and Mutriku lies the neighbourhood of San Jeronimo. In the fall of 2005 I wrote a column in the newspaper titled "San Jeronimo." In it I told how once when I was young I went with my parents to the San Jeronimo neighbourhood fair. When I was a teenager. September 30th is the feast day and every year it rains. "San Jeronimo the pisspot" the people in town call him because of it. The thing is, that time I went with my parents the accordionist Kaxiano was playing in the neighbourhood's small square. At the entrance a woman handed me a card, as she did all the kids. She had two decks of cards and dealt them out to the boys from one deck and to the girls from the other. You were supposed to dance with the person who had the same card as your own. One huge dilemma. Unable to overcome my shyness, I tossed my own lucky card in a corner and ended up not dancing with anyone at all.

I wondered who the girl was who'd been left cooling her heels waiting with the same card as mine. And whether she'd found love since then, or was even now cooling her heels, wondering when the boy with the card would show up.

That was what I told about in the column.

It came out in the fall of 2005. One night that winter Nerea said to me, "I was the girl who had the same card as you in San Jeronimo."

We've been together ever since.

Every summer without fail, the Bastidas used to make the same trip, at the beginning of June. Having rented a bus, they'd all climb in and set out for Ondarroa, the whole family and the maids as well. Images of the bus, too, turn up in the sixteen-millimetre short films that Bastida himself shot. In the old-style nineteen-twenties images there is the cabriolet-style bus and, in it, the architect's children, laughing, their hair blowing in the breeze.

They'd arrive in June and in September make the return trip. They spent the whole summer on the seacoast. Bastida was a methodical fellow, and the family's daily life was orderly too. They'd get up early in the morning and go to Mass, then from there to the beach, and around three go to have dinner. "Your father and his brothers, too, often came with us to eat at the house. Once they'd finished their chores on the beach. Your grandfather often spent time at our place as well," Carmen Bastida said. "I remember how one winter day he turned up at our house in Bilbao with an enormous hake. We were flabbergasted. 'The fact is, I remembered you-all.' That was what he said," she told us.

In the afternoon they'd do the housework. On weekends, go fishing in the river.

They went to church at seven in the morning. "We weren't too pleased about going to seven-o'clock Mass, that was too early for us," Carmen went on. "But we were thankful at the same time to have got up so early, especially during the town feast days, because if you went to eleven-o'clock

33

Mass, the big-heads would be lying in wait for the children outside when it got out. And I was very scared of the big-heads."

Bastida himself remained at home until 1 P.M., working, reading the press from abroad or listening to music. He had a gramophone in the living room and a quantity of recordings as well. "His favorite music of all was Wagner's."

He did his work at a big chestnut-wood table, he produced all his designs right there. "This was the table he worked at," Carmen told us, stroking it. We were having coffee at that same table, and it was there that Carmen had spread out the albums of black-and-white photographs.

Nerea and I had gone to visit Carmen at the house in Bilbao. It was unchanged since Ricardo Bastida had lived there, it felt as if the architect might open the street door and walk right in. His workplace was just as he'd left it. Painter friends' gifts hanging on the walls. Among them, works by Arteta. The sketches he'd made on paper for the Bank of Bilbao in Madrid.

Around 1 P.M. Bastida would show up on the beach. Always dressed in a suit. He'd take off the jacket and pass the time in his white dress shirt. There he'd be, in the shade, talking with friends. Carmen told us there was a saying around town about the white dress shirt.

"That Bastida, either he's way too clean or he's a filthy pig. Either he changes that shirt every single day or he wears that selfsame shirt day in and day out."

Since he invariably wore a white dress shirt.

"It goes without saying that he changed the shirt every day," Carmen added with a smile, and sat back.

"Do you remember what you liked best of that whole time?" I asked her after a brief silence.

"The taste of the strawberry ice creams. In June we'd pick mountain strawberries and then go for ice to the ice-house at the harbor. We'd gather the strawberries, get hold of the ice and make the ice cream at home. I will never, ever forget that taste."

The happiest day of all was the fifteenth of August, the day of the Blessed Virgin. It was Ondarroa's feast day and was also Ricardo Bastida's birthday. All the kids in town went to the Bastidas' country house that day, since Ricardo handed out sweets and whatnot to all the kids.

Bastida loved the cinema. In keeping with that, in the twenties he began making movies. Some were fictional, and others recorded the family's own daily habits. "Papa used to drive us mad – at first making movies was nice, we'd dress up in costumes and we felt like artistes. But then, all of it had to get organised, scenes gotten ready, takes shot over and over again. Even today I'm shocked at all the work that Papa put into it. And all to be doing something with his children," Carmen said of the movies.

Starting with the oldest and down to the newest we watched these films. *Sea Folk* was the first we saw.

Bastida Films
AGFA 16mm
1928

It was about the people of the seacoast, how the fishermen go about their work in the worst of conditions. He'd filmed the loss of a boat, storm and all. It looked real, even though he'd used a little toy whaler for the special effects. They filmed it on the Sagustan fishing ground, between Ondarroa and Lekeitio, directly across from Irabaltza Rock. The actors were the Bastidas and their children. Also the household help.

The second movie had a rural setting, *Jose Mari's Sandals,* filmed at an actual *baserri,* complete with a yoke of oxen. The third was a comedy, *Doctor Patakoff,* about a mad doctor.

After these came the films that depicted the family's daily life. Bathing at Arrigorri Beach. Ricardo, the eldest of the architect's sons, showed up, swimming off the strand there. "He was a graceful boy, an architect, he died in the war."

"He took a trip with his father to the United States when he was a boy –" I blurted out. I had read it in the architect's biography.

"That's exactly right. He was only fourteen. They crossed the Atlantic and spent time in New York, Chicago, Detroit and elsewhere. Papa had him write a daily diary of the trip. It's no big thing, kid stuff, children's stories."

The news of the diary made me gasp with surprise. I went to ask her something, but Carmen had her eyes on the movie.

"Look, Atano the Third."

It was true. Atano III was on the screen. Playing a game of handball at the town fronton without removing his beret. Next we saw scenes of the bicycle race coming along the Lekeitio road, the prowess of the great cyclist Barruetabeña.

Just after that, the children themselves – getting out of bed in the morning, taking their midday meal seated on wickerwork chairs, the girls' hair covered with mantillas. The day the son Jose Mari put on long trousers for the first time.

As the years go by, the way the children look goes on changing. From black-and-white images to images in colour. Carmen herself appears as a baby, Carmen as an older girl in Doña Casilda Park in Bilbao, Carmen as a young woman at the country house in summer. Those colour prints are the last. The very last are of a family portrait, with the maidservants in the garden.

In the foreground are Ricardo and Rosario, husband and wife. Aged now. One thing drew my attention, a gesture between them. At a certain point, husband and wife are gazing at each other, they stand quite close together. For a moment it looks as if they're going to give each other a kiss. But Rosario gives Ricardo a tap on the nose with the tip of a finger. Her husband smiles back at her.

"My life was changed by two events. The first blow was the war. The second was Papa's death."

I sat looking at Carmen. She was on in years now, but her large eyes were those of a girl. Our dad always wanted to pay Carmen a visit, from time to time our mother would say to him they ought to go see her and share childhood stories. But he never did. Now I was the one sitting before this woman.

Dad was startled the day I took up the atlas and a ballpoint pen and went in to him. It wasn't long after he'd retired from fishing.

I handed him the pen so he could draw the exact route they used to take to Rockall. He looked leery, as if another boat captain had asked him for one of his maritime secrets, the way to some hidden fishing ground.

He did it at last: Pass France, go up St. George's Channel and head northwest. That was the way to get to Rockall.

As I watched his nervous hand drawing, a strange sensation came over me. I understood that the mark Dad made with the ballpoint pen would remain in that atlas forever.

But at the same time something told me that he himself was not going to be around forever, the mark in the book was forever but Dad was not. I felt fear, a terror at losing my father.

A boat's captain never shows his navigational charts to anyone, when he goes ashore he rolls them up and takes them home with him.

Death doesn't show us its charts either.

5

HOUSEHOLD MATTERS

A writer needs protection. Especially at the beginning. He wants to gain confidence, to hear from outside that he's on the right track, hasn't made the wrong decision at that last crossroads. A writer needs protection when he's beginning. That's why I asked my father's opinion when I published my first column in the newspaper, to get his approval. Those columns were the first writing I ever published, back in far-off 1998. My beginnings. That first column was terrifically worked over, the outcome of long hours of writing. In the effort to write as well as I could possibly write, it ended up being something more like a short short story. But I've realised since then that short stories are short stories and columns columns. Because columns have an essential characteristic that short stories don't: extemporaneousness.

Dad's was no run-of-the-mill response. I didn't get his approval. On the contrary, he answered by way of a story. When he was a teenager, he said, there had been two priests in town. Each had his own, familiar way of preaching a sermon. One of them was colloquial, intimate, Don Manuel, people took in the things he had to say with ease. The style

of the other priest, though, was tortuous. Nobody understood a thing he said. Dad was speaking of Don Jesus. He
addressed his sermons to the rich people who sat in the front
pews, taking no account of the people farther back. So, I was
writing in the manner of that second priest, Dad said, in the
style of Don Jesus, with a poker face.

I will always be thankful to my father for that honesty.
On the one hand he revealed to me that what I'd written
was way too literary for the pages of a newspaper. And, on
the other, he didn't give me a direct opinion, didn't say "The
column is good" or "It's bad." He clothed his argument in a
story, making no direct evaluations. That's what I liked best,
I mean, that because of that story of his I saw everything
more clearly. In fact, it's stories that contain the shadings
and details of reality. And it's the details that are what's
most important in life.

It's weird the way memory works, how we remember in
our own way, turning what at one time was presumably reality into fiction. It works that way in families especially. To
remember the people who came before us, their stories get
told, and from those anecdotes we know what that person
was like. Roles get assigned to us and people remember us
according to those roles.

Of my mother's grandmother, people say she was a very
pious woman. Grandma Susana wore long skirts, and she

even drank vinegar to make her face paler, as a mortification of her beauty. At Christmastime each year she'd set up a large nativity scene at her house. She used the whole parlour for it. She herself, by hand, made the wax figures for the scene, she made the shepherds and the sheep, she made the saints. She shaped mountains out of moss and there was even a little river, with real water.

The people in town had the custom of visiting our grandmother's house, parents and children would go to see Susana's display. As they left the house they'd drop a few coins in the little basket that had pictures of an acolyte on it.

That's how Grandma Susana would make a bit of money. That and dressing up the saints in the church. Her special concern was the Mother of Sorrows. She laundered the clothing of the statue of the Blessed Virgin. Once an accident took place. In July of 1908 there was a disaster at sea. The town fishermen, terrified, gave a sum of money to the church, so that nothing of the kind would happen again. With that money they made a new mantle for the Mother of Sorrows. And Susana took the old mantle for herself and put it away in a trunk. Our grandma Anparo, her daughter, asked her what she needed that mantle for. "When I die, I want you to lay me out in this mantle." Her daughter couldn't believe it. It drove her crazy when Susana would take the old mantle from the trunk and hang it on the balcony, if there was a south wind. "The mantle's got to be kept aired out, for the big day" was Susana's regular response.

I heard of that terrible 1908 disaster from Aunt Maritxu, in fact, who told me of it when I went to visit her at her home up in Begoña. She said that her grandfather Canuto and uncle Ignacio had drowned right in the bay of Ondarroa, and that they never did find the bodies. The household had seen the boat going down from quite nearby, she told me, but were unable to do a thing. The family's watching had made what was itself tragic all the more harrowing.

Maritxu hadn't yet been born when the disaster took place. She, too, would have been told about what happened, at home growing up most probably. And she passed it on to me, too, just as she'd heard it, as if she'd lived through it close-up too.

But when I went to the justice of the peace for Canuto and Ignacio Badiola's death certificates, I was dumbstruck. Marta had the papers waiting for me. The memoranda recording the first news of Canuto's death were right there too. But one datum threw me. Grandfather Canuto and the rest of them didn't die in the bay of Ondarroa, but instead way over off the coast of Santander.

I looked at contemporary news accounts later on and what turned up in them showed that the papers hadn't been mistaken: the boats had gone down off the coast of Santander. The news accounts gave details, too, the wind had suddenly shifted to the northwest and the sailboats went down on the spot.

Twenty-eight souls died in all on that twelfth of July in 1908. From the *San Marcos* seven, from the *San Jeronimo* eight, from the *Santa Margarita* two, from the *Jesus Maria & Jose* three, from the *Nuestra Señora de la Antigua* three, from the *Concepción* four and from the *San Ignacio* only one.

They were able to get the sloop *San Jeronimo* to the surface, the steamer *Joaquín de Bustamante* was plying the waters there, searching, and that's how they discovered her.

But how could Maritxu tell me the boat was lost in Ondarroa? Why the relocation?

The tragedy had been so huge that when they remembered it they even changed the place of death. They brought it nearer, from Santander to Ondarroa. Memory brought the bitterness closer.

It's interesting to see how collective memory does its work. The case of the Berriozabal fountain in Elorrio is a demonstration of this. Down through the generations it's been thought that the fountain depicted Incan motifs.

It was Manuel Berriozabalgoitia who caused the fountain to be built in the nineteenth century. After studying

law he'd gone to Peru and thereabouts; he reached Cuzco
in 1803. He met a Creole woman there: Maria. Dark-haired,
with large eyes, themselves dark, sad, as if the burden of the
world were too much for them. Maria was of a good family. One of the richest in Peru. Her parents didn't want that
unknown quantity Manuel Berriozabalgoitia in their house,
this young lawyer just off the boat from Europe. Four years
later the couple were married. The boy was smart, and pru-
dent. In a few short years, he had multiplied Maria's family's
holdings, to his father-in-law's surprise and joy. It appeared
that nothing was going to stand in their way. But all cloth
has an underside. Rebels rose up in Quito. And then in
Charcas and then in Potosí. Soon they would achieve inde-
pendence from Spain. Manuel and his companions, all their
holdings lost, found themselves obliged to return to Europe.

They say the Elorrio winters were too long for Maria.
That she didn't have someone to talk to, anyone to enjoy herself with. Her husband was intent on recovering his holdings
and spent long stretches away from home, in Madrid. And
Maria, when autumn was on its way, felt a deep affliction
come over her heart and she dwelt in her memory on the
sunny landscapes and noisy streets of Cuzco.

Maria changed. She was ever more silent. People saw her
walking in the forests round about, all alone. Even at meal-
times husband and wife didn't exchange a word.

That was when Manuel decided to build the fountain. That fountain would bring Cuzco before her, its light, the happy years he and Maria had spent there.

No sooner said than done. Miguel Elkoroberezibar drew up the design. They chose the area's best stonecutters. They chose the stones with great care, chiselled them with great care, and with great care laid one stone on top of another.

So goes the story that people still tell in Elorrio.

I liked that story about the fountain. For one thing, I liked the part about exile. Manuel and Maria, one or the other would be in exile, whichever place they lived in. One or the other would at some time have the yearning to return to their birthplace. Despite knowing that time changes places and peoples. And I especially liked someone's having done such a glorious thing to make their friend happy, having dared to make that final effort, to try to be again what they'd been before.

It's said that fantasy is based on reality, but the law of the story is to tell only one part of the truth. That's how it has to be. Otherwise it doesn't work. And that's how I learned that the story of the fountain had taken very little from real life.

Miguel Elkoroberezibar knew less than nothing about Peruvian art and based his design for the fountain on another school entirely: the neoclassical. Manuel Berriozabalgoitia's plan wasn't romantic at all. It was progress Manuel believed in, and he built the fountain to improve the living conditions of the neighbourhood.

All the rest is people's fantasy.

6

TWO FRIENDS

As we were saying our goodbyes, Carmen Bastida put a packet into my hands. "This is Papa's correspondence with Arteta," she said. "I hope you find something of value in it. They're for you, there's no need to return it."

They were photocopies of the original letters, since she'd known I'd be visiting, and also that I was running down traces of Bastida and Arteta's relationship, she'd had the packet ready. She didn't give it to me, however, until just as we were saying goodbye.

"Don't fret. Your grandparents were good people," she said as she came up to kiss me goodbye. It set me thinking. The next day, I opened the packet and began to look through the letters Arteta and Bastida had written each other. Unfortunately, there were no letters from the time of the country-house mural and their work on the Bank of Bilbao. A bit later I learned that while construction was going on in Madrid, Bastida paid Arteta a weekly visit there. And so there was no need for letters. The letters were from later.

The business in Madrid turned out as they'd thought it would. They had a huge success. As a result, the two artists worked together on a number of other projects. The first, at the Bilbao secondary school.

It was 1927. On the first of October the first public secondary school in downtown Bilbao would be opening, and they wanted a portrait of King Alfonso XIII for the occasion. Bastida had designed the school and he remembered his friend Arteta then too. Arteta finished the painting in good time, and on the day of note they hung the picture in the school's auditorium.

After the war, though, it was lost, without a trace. And that's how it appears in the art books as well, as a missing picture.

In the spring of 2005 I was at that very school, giving a talk. In that very auditorium. Almost as soon as I entered the hall I realised that there, smack in the middle of the wall, was the painting. I couldn't believe it.

"You've got a jewel here," I told the students and teachers, amazed, since I, too, had believed all trace of the painting to have been lost.

One of the teachers, hearing this, told me the painting's history.

"It hasn't always hung in the same place," the teacher said. "Not long ago, in among the worm-eaten tables and chairs in the storeroom, they unearthed a large canvas. The picture was of Franco, painted in the nineteen-forties. As they began cleaning it they realised there was another image painted underneath. Once the top coat was gone, they met up with the face of Alfonso XIII."

It was Arteta's painting. During all those years the painting hadn't left the school, it had been right there, but under another image.

Franco the dictator, you could say, overlay all things.

The second commission they collaborated on was the seminary of Logroño. Bastida proposed to Arteta that he paint the pictures to decorate the Logroño seminary.

For Arteta the job was hell on earth. The bishop in charge of the seminary didn't have too much faith in the agnostic painter and he wouldn't leave him alone. Arteta had a bad time of it, and that comes across in the letters. But they have their comic side as well.

Reading these letters you see clear as day what Arteta and Bastida were like. They were totally different from one another. Arteta wrote his letters by hand. He'd take a half-sheet and fold it. He'd start his letter on the front, then fill the inside, and finish up on the back. If there was a mistake, he'd just cross it out and go on.

Bastida's letters bear no relation. They're an entirely different thing. They're typewritten, immaculate, and have no crossings out. No matter what, he wrote using carbon paper, to keep a copy at home of the letters he'd written.

The pages themselves are elegant. At the top on the left they have a printed letterhead.

RICARDO DE BASTIDA
ARCHITECT

Ondárroa (Biscay)
Telephone No. 1

The great majority of the times, Arteta was writing to Bastida to ask for help. For instance, when he has to present to the bishop the projected design he'd come up with, he asks the architect to take his side. And he's writing to complain as well, that the bishop is meddling in his work too much.

It does seem the bishop would not leave Arteta in peace, he was always bringing him church books and holy cards to show him and Arteta was on the verge of going insane. The bishop kept showing him little holy cards and telling him he wanted it to look like this saint or the other.

"The man does not realise that illustrations are one thing and painting is another," Arteta would tell Bastida in a fury. What's more, the bishop wanted the Virgin Mother to go in the very center of the mural, as if it were an outsize holy card.

The letter Bastida sent Arteta on May 23, 1929, is memorable.

Bastida tells Arteta to hold fast, to pay no attention to what the bishop has said. If once he does, for instance in the matter of positioning the Virgin Mother, it will be the ruin of the picture. For from that point on, he will always and perpetually have to do what the bishop wants. Hold on, Bastida tells him, please hold on, if the bishop sees him sticking to his guns, he'll leave him in peace and not meddle further in his work. Something of the same kind happened to Bastida himself, he says, when he presented the plans for the building, but finally the bishop simply had to approve them and the subject was closed, after a long hard fight.

> Though it may be difficult for you, rein in your refinement. Forgive my stating things so clearly: what's right is not giving way when your artistic conscience is wounded, but persevering. If you don't, if you give way for the sake of being pleasant, you will regret having done so for the rest of your life, it will be a millstone around your conscience. Once

again, don't take my words' crudeness amiss: if you fail to win this first battle, everything will go downhill.

Your good friend sends regards with the greatest pleasure,

Bastida

The architect's letter, however, wasn't forceful enough. On June 8th, writing from Logroño, Arteta confesses to Bastida that he gave way to the bishop. He says he'll be putting the Virgin Mother in the very center but that it won't be so bad that way. In primitive painting, too, it was done in just such a way and so is going to be based on that.

But Arteta was trying to deceive himself.

Bastida knew all too well what would happen. On the first of October the work was supposed to be done, but in the letter Arteta wrote on September 4th his despair is self-evident. There are many difficulties, he writes. The marble dust is not as fine as what he'd used in Madrid and the water, too, is not to his liking. It dries too fast. His money is running out as well and he asks Bastida if there might be some way to get a portion of the payment before the work's been finished.

After all that time he's painted nothing but the mural's horizon line.

My dear Bastida:

You will be alarmed to learn that work is so far behindhand. But matters began to take an ugly turn when I started painting the image of the Virgin Mother. I've done it over four times. A few times because I myself didn't like it, and the rest because of the bishop. These last-minute changes have snarled up the work mightily.

Look, the first head I painted the bishop did like, but he told me it seemed small to him, skimpy, and went on to inform me of the importance of the image of the Virgin Mother, by way of a deeply pious diatribe.

I had no recourse but to make it larger. The outcome finally didn't seem to me all that bad, since in primitive painting, too, one image is frequently larger than another. But the matter didn't stop there. When he realised that the Virgin Mother was larger than the apostles he told me, "It's not good for male figures to be smaller than female ones," and he added, "You will be able to make those images larger, won't you?"

It doesn't matter to me in the least if I go over this and correct it a hundred times, but it gripes my soul that on top of making a mess of the work,

the bishop doesn't even conceive of the effort I
put in. Moreover, this past week, I took sick.
With warm regards and an embrace,
Arteta

Though it's hard to believe, Arteta did at last finish the work and, what's more, everyone liked it. Even the bishop himself. The critics praised his gestures at primitivism, saying they brought to mind the murals of Fra Angelico.

There was, however, at least one critic on hand to emphasise Arteta's lack of faith, and to say that Arteta hadn't actually believed in the whole endeavor.

Both Arteta's doubts and his lack of security reminded me of my own novel and its writing process.

I wrote the novel's first sentence in December of 2002.

I wanted a powerful sentence to start off the novel, a sentence like the one that opens Carson McCullers's *The Heart Is a Lonely Hunter.* "In the town there were two mutes, and they were always together." That sentence says a lot. It tells us that the novel will be about two mutes, and it illuminates the two mutes' marginalisation too. And also the camaraderie they share.

Or the opening sentence of Sylvia Plath's *The Bell Jar.* "It was a queer, sultry summer, the summer they electrocuted the Rosenbergs, and I didn't know what I was doing in New York." A marvellous opening. In a single sentence the story is situated, when and where and how the narrator stands.

"By the time my father was born the house was in ruins."

That was the sentence I chose as the beginning of my novel. Later I erased the words "my father" and it ended up "By the time he was born they had razed the house to the ground." I thought "By the time he was born" really had something going for it, that it would pique a reader's curiosity.

I even applied for a grant for the novel project that very year, with that sparkling opening sentence of mine, but they rejected it. I titled the project "Two Friends," and it wouldn't make it much past twenty-odd pages.

Out of those twenty pages, there was only a single sentence in that first draft that was worth giving a thought to.

"Houses do die if nobody lives in them, and people do too."

When they rejected it I was sad, I have to admit. But here and now I'm thankful for the good sense of that jury. It was too early back then to write the book, things do have their own season.

Nevertheless, I've got to say that I held on to that 2002 beginning, I left it unchanged for a long, long time. I even made a bet with friends, that I'd hang on to that sentence until the novel was done. But, on the other hand, I felt that would be a bad sign, I wouldn't get very far along hanging on to the same sentence.

I finally do lose the bet, as on so many other occasions, and do change the opening sentence.

"Fish and trees are alike."

7

FRANKFURT

So we get in to Frankfurt. Three-twenty in the afternoon.
The flight to New York leaves at five. I've got a mere hour
and forty minutes to get from Terminal B to Terminal A. We
didn't get a Jetway here. They take us to the terminal on a
bus. The glass doors open. The escalators take us upstairs.
Passport control. Down the elevator. The tunnel that goes
from one terminal to the other. The lights in the tunnel flash
on and off. Now red now green. There's also some music in
the air. A few random notes. It looks like a spaceship. Into
the elevator and I come out in Terminal A. Directly in front
of me is the screen that lists what gates the flights leave
from. I search out New York. New York. LH 404. It's Gate
A-32.

Security check for the United States of America. They
have me take off my shoes. I sit down in the waiting room.
It hasn't changed since the last time I went to New York.
Behind the plate glass are the airplanes. Settling down now,
I begin looking at the people. Looking at the people who
are going to be on the flight with me.

I remember when we went in 2003 I became aware of
a girl who had an Indian look about her. She was pacing

around. At one moment our eyes met, and held. She had huge dark eyes. Bashful. Then, she was lost in the crowd. As I was waiting for the moment we might finally get on the plane, passing the time, I wondered what that girl was going to New York to do. She'd be studying at New York University, maybe. She might have gone to India to visit her family and now was on her way back to the United States.

After waiting in line, I got on the plane and to my seat. I was putting my bag in the overhead bin and didn't even realise. The Indian girl was behind me, standing, with her boarding pass in her hand. Her seat was the one next to mine. I had a pleasant surprise, in fact it was a huge coincidence, on a plane that had over three hundred seats, the two of us ending up next to each other. She didn't say a word. With a tight smile, she put her things in the overhead bin, sat down, and fastened her seat belt. Boarding completed. They closed the doors of the plane.

At the outset I didn't dare to say anything to her. I thought seven hours would be enough to begin getting acquainted. Once we were airborne a conversation would come up on its own.

We were in seats in the plane's middle rows. In the most uncomfortable place, since it's not easy to get out, stretch your legs if you want to, or if you need to go to the bathroom.

The girl realised that the two seats by the window were free and asked the flight attendant if she could go sit over there. The flight attendant told her yes. Another tight smile as a goodbye to me. And the alleged Indian girl went to sit by the window, leaving the seat next to mine vacant.

But the thing didn't end there. Not five minutes later, a man went and stood next to her. Was the seat free. The girl nodded her head yes, as if in distress. At the same time, a man sat down next to me as well. Central European.

Once the plane was in the air, the guy beside me took a few magazines out of the bag he had between his feet. They were fashion magazines. He opened one and began to tear out the pages. Vigorously too. He did that during the entire flight. Ripping out the pages one by one, again and again. He crumpled all these pages and discarded them into the bag. In a very violent way.

I couldn't even get any sleep. Thinking the guy could, with the same force he was ripping out pages with, wring my neck.

The guy next to the girl, meanwhile, didn't shut up the whole flight. He kept asking her questions and acted as if he was courting her or something. The girl didn't pay him much attention. Once she looked straight at me across the seats. As if to say she'd made a bad choice. That was the second look that passed between us, and the last.

She gathered up her stuff and went somewhere farther forward.

We didn't run into each other again. Our lives united in that one moment and then each life went its own way. As if they were two great rivers that almost touch each other, in their long windings.

Our aunt Margarita, Mum's sister, used to tell us when we were little that Dad had once lost his wedding ring in the ocean and that she herself had found it in the belly of a hake, at the kitchen sink in our house, when she was cleaning the hake. That was the unlikeliest of all coincidences that could ever come to pass. For Dad to lose his ring at sea, for a hake to eat it, and for that hake to be caught by our father's boat. And out of all the hundreds of hake that had been caught, for our dad to choose that single hake, and for it to be the one that had swallowed his wedding ring. I don't know what the exact numerical probability would be of something like that happening, but I am certain the chance is infinitesimal. What's worse is that even now Aunt periodically swears to me it's true, that it actually happened.

I wrote a poem about all this, too, with the title "The Gold Ring." When the poem was published something happened that I didn't expect. I got a number of email messages, sent from all over the place, telling of similar things that had happened. All of them had to do with lost gold rings, and how they were found after many years had passed, in the most unbelievable ways. One of my friends even called me on the phone to say he'd seen Tim Burton's *Big Fish* and in that film, too, a large fish swallows a gold ring and couldn't it be that Tim Burton had copied the story in my poem.

The most sensible message, though, was the one from the Deusto University oral-literature professor Jabier Kaltzakorta.

From: Jabier Kaltzakorta, kaltzakorta@deustu.edu
To: Kirmen Uribe, kirmen@gmail.com
Date: 04-11-2004
Subject: the gold ring

Because of what your aunt recounts, I'm writing to tell you that the story of the gold ring is a legend widespread throughout the whole of Europe. You'll recall, for example, the narrative the great Italo Calvino collected in his *Six Memos for the Next Millennium,* in his lecture on quickness, as it happens:

Late in life, the emperor Charlemagne fell in love with a German girl. The barons at his court were extremely worried when they saw that the sovereign, wholly taken up with his amorous passion and unmindful of his regal dignity, was neglecting the affairs of state. When the girl suddenly died, the courtiers were greatly relieved – but not for long, because Charlemagne's love did not die with her. The emperor had the embalmed body carried to his bedchamber, where he refused to be parted from it.

The Archbishop Turpin, alarmed by this macabre passion, suspected an enchantment and insisted on examining the corpse. Hidden under the girl's dead tongue he found a ring with a precious stone set in it. As soon as the ring was in Turpin's hands, Charlemagne fell passionately in love with the archbishop and hurriedly had the girl buried. In order to escape the embarrassing situation, Turpin flung the ring into Lake Constance. Charlemagne thereupon fell in love with the lake and would not leave its shores.

That's Calvino's version, collected in Italy. The ring is the crux of the story. Nonetheless, it has differences from your variation. Although the ring itself does, the fish doesn't appear anywhere at all in Calvino's.

Because of that, I'd say the work of Herodotus is the most direct source for the gold ring. Herodotus wrote his *Histories* in the fifth century B.C. or so, and collected in it many, many things from contemporary oral culture. This, among them:

There once was a king named Polycrates in the isles of Greece. Polycrates had great good fortune in his life, and said as much to Amasis, his Egyptian ally, in a letter. Polycrates told him he was happy in his life, he had no complaint, he had nothing further to ask of life, except to continue just as he was. Amasis got angry with him. Obviously angry as well. And Amasis told Polycrates it was reckless of him to say he was happy, that such a thing could do nothing but make for envy in his surroundings. And Amasis gave Polycrates a piece of advice, that being happy wasn't enough, he had to undergo suffering, too. And therefore, to wit, in order to suffer, he had to lose the thing he loved the most.

Polycrates pondered this at length but finally determined to follow his friend's advice. He took a gold ring a dear friend had given him and threw it into the sea, so as to learn what loss was. The ring, however, was swallowed by a large fish and a fisherman caught that fish. The fisherman, seeing the size of the fish, was moved to offer it to King Polycrates as a gift, Polycrates being such a good man.

When the fish was cleaned, Polycrates quickly saw that that ring was his own, that fate had brought the ring home to him. And he decided that it was the command of the Gods, that the Gods meant to tell him that suffering for nothing was not worth it, life itself would bring suffering enough on its own, and if he was happy it was up to him to continue being happy.

From the Middle Ages onward, the story Herodotus wrote was picked up in the lives of the saints. The legend of Saint Attilanus of Zamora tells that the saint threw his ring into the Duero River when he left his birthplace and set out for Jerusalem. He wanted to pay for the sins of his youth in that way, having done penance. The saint believed that if the ring reappeared at some time, that would be a sign from God. A sign of forgiveness. At the end of a few years when he returned to his birthplace, they gave the saint the gift of a fish. In the fish he found his ring.

If your grandmother Susana was as pious as you say, it could well be that your aunt heard the story from her own grandmother. Who can tell.

Our aunt Margarita was born during the war, in 1937. The second of five sisters. Even her name speaks worlds. Grandma Anparo named her first daughter Ane Miren, a Basque name, in the time of the Republic. She left her second daughter's naming to her mother-in-law, however. The two of them had been furious for ages because of politics. The mother-in-law was a traditionalist and our grandmother was a nationalist. To calm the waters and get their relationship on a better footing she told her mother-in-law that she herself would be picking the name for the baby. Her mother-in-law, however, was not so forgiving. She called the baby Margarita, the name of the traditionalists' ladies auxiliary, to piss our grandmother off. And that's how our aunt became Margarita forever.

Her generation was perhaps the one that underwent the most changes. Raised in the straitened society of the postwar, they suddenly had to fathom the ideas of the '68 revolution. Mum herself has said to me more than once, they went from working in Christian communities to being Marxists in just a few months. It was no commonplace evolution. From morning to night, she said, everything from before became useless for anything.

But inside them the two worlds were both very much alive. And precisely because of that, even though Aunt Margarita was the trade-union rep at the cannery, she herself took care of setting up the nativity scene at Christmastime and would take us up to the Antigua hermitage on foot, and tell us that one of the images in the hermitage, that of the Nazarene, was miraculous. The image of the Nazarene sits in a vitrine below the choir loft of the church of La Antigua. If you give the saint in the vitrine a kiss with your hand, Aunt Margarita used to tell us, it enlightens your mind. And so, when I had a test coming up she'd take me there to give a kiss with my hand, even though I hadn't been baptised. And that's how I carried on with the habit in secondary school, and even in college, when exams had me overwhelmed.

I don't know if Aunt truly believed in those miraculous powers of the Nazarene, just as I don't know if she was truly and seriously saying she'd found Dad's wedding ring in the belly of a hake. Most certainly: not. But I don't care, these stories themselves are the most important thing, whether they're true or false.

8

THE FOURTEEN-YEAR-OLD BOY

A month after Nerea and I spent time with Carmen Bastida, a packet came in the mail. Sent by Carmen herself. In it was a small ring binder. On the notebook's cover "My Trip to the Chicago Eucharistic Congress. June and July, 1926" was printed.

It was the diary of young Ricardo Bastida, the architect's son and namesake. It was of a size to carry around with you, six inches by three. The covers were cardboard and the pages were ruled. It held eighty-six pages in all. Ricardo himself had numbered them. Of the eighty-six pages, eighty-four were written on. Bastida's handwriting was that of any fourteen-year-old.

Carmen had guessed when my curiosity was piqued at her mention of young Ricardo's daily diary. Still, I'd thought at the time that that journal would probably be an intimate thing, and so hadn't insisted on asking to see it.

And now look, without my saying a word, Carmen herself had put it into my hands.

Along with it came a little note: "They're only children's stories, kid stuff, but just in case. Carmen."

—

I'm sitting waiting, cooling my heels until boarding gets started at Gate A-32, and I take young Ricardo's journal out of my bag. This human who, eighty-two years earlier, took the same trip I'm about to take, the voyage I have to make by air, he made by ship.

The journal begins on June 3, 1926. "Before starting our trip, on the third of June, since it's Corpus Christi Day, I took Communion in Ondarroa church and asked God for a good journey and a fruitful one." That's Ricardo's opening sentence.

That first day, they spent the whole day in San Sebastian and, after saying goodbye to his mother and his brother Juan Luis, they took the train to Hendaye. Juan Luis had been all set to go to the United States, too, but hadn't gotten grades as good as Ricardo did that term. But then, Ricardo had got A's in everything, and so wouldn't be charged tuition next year.

While they were in Hendaye, the architect and his son paid a call on Unamuno. Young Ricardo records the moment this way:

"Papa talked with a man who's named Miguel de Unamuno and is banished for speaking evil of the king and Primo de Rivera."

He sets down nothing more than that. It could be the boy didn't know that much about who this blessed Unamuno was anyway. His father might have told him to write something about Unamuno in the journal, because he was a great man.

As Ricardo noted correctly, the writer Miguel de Unamuno was in exile in Hendaye. He was writing the novel *How to Write a Novel* at the time. In one passage of the book he tells about visits from the south side of the border. He recounts that when people come to visit him they ask him how long the dictatorship is going to last. His answer normally is this: "How long will it last? As long as you want it to last."

Before leaving for Hendaye, young Ricardo and his brother Juan Luis and their parents had gone to Igeldo Park. There they spent some pleasurable moments before saying their goodbyes to each other at Atotxa train station. Ricardo was heartsick and set it down in his journal in so many words.

We used to go to Igeldo Park, too, when we were little, when our dad came in from sea. Once, we got into the dinghies there and Dad tried to teach us how to row. At one point a man nearby came alongside and asked him, "You wouldn't be Jose Uribe, would you?"

Dad's jaw dropped, because he'd never seen the man in his life. "I knew you by your voice," the man said. "I'm a captain myself and I recognised your voice from the radiophone." It was their custom on the fishing boats to switch on the radiophone and listen in on what the other captains were saying, to find out where the fishing was that day.

I turn back to Ricardo's diary.

June 4

We're in Paris now. I've seen Napoleon's tomb, a panoramic display about the great war, and after seeing a lot of other things I went with Papa up to the third level of the Eiffel tower. From there the view is glorious but I was scared to look down. I sailed a paper aeroplane off the top of the tower.

I look out through the plate glass yet again. The bags are coming by on the little loading carts. Then the workers send them into the hold on a set of conveyor belts. I keep a lookout for my own among the hundreds of bags. Impossible.

They've called for boarding. The people in the first rows have to board first. My seat is 49C. I'll have to wait.

June 6

At Cherbourg we got on the ocean liner. This steamship Aquitania is like a whole town, a lot bigger than the Palace hotel in Madrid. Just the seamen and the service crew add up to 1,000 people. It's got spectacular salons and galleries with long promenades. They're so long you get tired out when you run from one end to the other. Often they play music or orchestra. There's a pool to swim in, a hall to exercise in with lots of equipment, and on the boat deck they play lots of games. They're easy and fun, when we get back we'll have to play them in Ondarroa.

It's the turn of the rear seats now. After waiting in line I get on the aircraft. The plane's service crew say hello. *Guten Abend.* The aircraft is a custom-built model, brand-new. An Airbus 340-600. It's got something upwards of three hundred seats and it's clear there's more space between the rows. I suddenly realise that there are no toilets in the usual places. In the plane's midsection are several small stairways going down to a lower level. That's where the toilets are. I get to my seat. 49C. On the aisle.

I pull out Bastida's notebook and stow my bag in the overhead bin. I settle in to read.

June 7
The time of day. When we got on the ship in Cherbourg we turned the time back one hour

to be on the sun's time, and then every night we have to turn the clock back 50 minutes. That way when we reach New York, from the six nights we spend on the crossing we'll have turned back the time of day by 6 x 50 = 300 minutes, which means a 5 hour change from the meridian.

Onboard movies. At 5 in the afternoon we had movies in one of the ship salons. The movie was very boring but these North Americans laughed and laughed like little kids.

It's clear how young Bastida got his A in math. It's weird to see what sort of thing he jotted down in his notebook. The time-change business, for instance. How science stuff gets interesting at that age. The world is wide open when you're fourteen. He lays out intelligence about the ocean liner's daily life. All the details: how every day they hose down the lifeboats, to make sure the joins are tight since the boats are wooden, so they won't go down in any hypothetical crisis. How the women onboard wear their hair short and eyeglasses. Which people will be going on to Chicago with them for the eucharistic congress. "Monsignor Leiper, the head of the Council of Ministers of Austria, spends the whole day reading and has a bullet in his body from an assassination attempt."

Bastida mentions a five-hour time change between Cherbourg and New York. Nowadays there's a six-hour difference. What they did in six days, we'll do in seven and a half hours. On the small screen on the seatback in front of me come the details of the journey.

> Distance to Destination: 3,800 miles
> Time to destination: 7:30 hours
> Local Time: 11:42 AM
> Ground Speed: 0 mph
> Altitude: 0
> Outside air temperature: 59° F

The plane is filling up. A fat fellow sits down across the aisle from me. In front of me, though, a few young people have taken their seats. They look northern European from their jerseys; on the three boys' shirts it says "North Sea Jazz Festival. Rotterdam." Members of a music group, maybe.

June 8
We saw the second-class and third-class rooms, they're all right but in the third-class rooms there was a bad smell and a great deal of noise.

I saw dolphins that were trying to catch the steamship today and also a bird, like a kind of large swallow, it must have been 1,500 miles from land.

I start thinking over what bird that must have been. Whether it could possibly have been a cormorant, or common shag.

The shag, or cormorant, is a special kind of seabird. In wintertime it flies in close to the cliffs along the Cantabrian seacoast. People also call it a sea crow, because it's pitch-black. You can tell a shag/cormorant by its long neck. In actual fact, and if you pay attention to what the fishermen say, it's been years and years since the bird has appeared in our area, apparently because of the pollution on the Cantabrian coast.

The shag makes its home in Ireland and Scotland and the cold of winter brings it down to us. It's a protected species. Along the Basque coast only seventy-some mating pairs live, at most. They take the same mate, too, their whole life long.

I didn't know what a shag was called in Ondarroa. Nerea said it was called a *sakillu,* at least that's what the kids in town called them. Shags can stay underwater a long time and when one dives the town kids have a game of guessing where in the water it will surface. When the bird breaks the surface of the water, she told me, the kids yell, *"Sakillu, sakillu!"*

But I was doubtful whether that wasn't another species. My wife and I couldn't manage to agree. Finally, to clear things up, I looked in Eneko Barrutia's *Biscayan Fishermen's Lexicon*.

> **Sakillo-sakillu (O-b), sakilluk (O-b)**
> Def: n. *Phalacrocorax Aristotelis*. Common shag.
> Sp. Cormorán Aud.: O-b: ~-s usually fly along
> the waterline.

Yet again, Nerea was right, the shag/cormorant was called a *sakillu*.

Nevertheless, that wasn't the end of it. I wondered what "(O-b)" meant. I looked in the *Lexicon*'s index of abbreviations.

> O-b = Ondarroa, Boni Laka

I was stunned when I read this, and also sad, since Boni Laka was our own uncle. Uncle Boni. He was the one who'd told Barrutia a shag was called a *sakillu*.

And I hadn't had a clue.

—

In the spring of 2006 I ran into Eneko Barrutia in Bilbao. At a talk I was giving. "Agirre's Roses," I'd called it.

When the formalities were over, he gave me a CD.

"These are the recordings I made of your uncle for the lexicon."

"Boni Laka Iturriza, 1-31-1997," it said on the jewel case. Uncle Boni was the husband of our mother's eldest sister, Ane Miren. He was an inshore sea captain all his life. *Bizkargi* was the name of his boat, the Humpback. I vividly remember the boat, painted in red, green and white. Even when there was a ban on those colours, Uncle wanted her painted just that way. Even if the Francoists brought a denunciation and he'd have to paint it out.

Uncle and the *Bizkargi* went together. When he got sick and was bedridden the boat, too, went down forever. A big iron-hulled vessel slammed into the old wooden *Bizkargi* when she was tied up in port. There was no way to fix the damage. The two of them, Uncle and the boat, quit navigating together.

I didn't listen to the recording right off. It made me feel diffident, the way we feel when we see someone we're close to and haven't seen for a long time. A few days later I put the CD in my iBook and listened to the first track. I was staggered. Uncle's voice wasn't at all the way it was when he was sick. You could hear the strength of the man.

One of the last memories I have of him was this: They sent him home from the hospital, telling him his life was now a matter of a few months. At home, we watched a pelota match on TV together. Even though all of us were looking at the television, Uncle didn't glance at it. Paying no attention to the ups and downs of the pelota players, during the whole match he had his eyes on us, contemplating the members of his family instead of the TV.

In the interviews done in order to make a dictionary, the very first necessity is to set the interviewee at ease, the person being interviewed has to be made to forget that someone's recording his voice. And so the questions at the outset are easy ones, a breeze to answer. For instance, he's asked when and where he was born.

That's what Professor Barrutia did with our uncle. He queried him first on when his birthday was and when he'd first gone to sea. He was born in September of 1928, Uncle told him, and he was only eight when the war hit and he had no way of going to school. He and his brother were the youngest at home, and their father and oldest brothers had fled the town, because they were nationalists. They were said to be staying in Bermeo, catching fish for the Basque fighting men on a boat called the *Our Father*. When the war ended and they came back to town, they were tried and banished, and Boni's father spent the years in Pasaia, working on draggers.

As the recording went along, there came a sentence that when he was alive he'd say only every once in a while, "Before the ocean was full of fish, now it's full of water." A sentence that declares the downfall of the fisheries, beyond a doubt. There might well be technology but there are no fish, because there's been too much fishing. Uncle says that at one time they used to fish by eye. You could see on the water's surface where the fish were, because of the foam or because of the sparkle. Then the machinery came.

How a dictionary gets made. I've often wondered. On the tape you can hear clearly what the technique is. Professor Barrutia says a word, most often in Spanish, and Uncle offers the local Basque word. For instance, when he asks *sotavento* ("leeward"), Uncle says *haixebekaldi,* and if Barrutia asks for *barlovento* ("windward"), *haixekaldi.*

On the CD Uncle says ever so many words I've never heard even once, myself, words from a lost lexicon, like *sakillu.*

But that's not the upshot. After the lexicographer's asked Uncle to translate a word, he tells him to put a "three" – *hiru* – in front of the translated word, so as to hear what the word sounds like without the definite article. For example, Uncle, having been asked what *vela* ("sail") is, will answer *"Beli."*

And with "three" in front of it?

Hiru bela.

And so it goes, with a whole slew of words. And when Barrutia asks him to translate *viento norte* ("norther") Uncle will tell him *haize franku.* But then the amusement begins. "How would you say *hiru haize –*" Barrutia goes on to ask him, automatically, and Uncle comes out with "You can't say *hiru haize franko,* man, there's no more northers than just the one of them!"

Recorded on the CD is the laughter of both men.

"Why do you keep saying 'three' over and over again?" Uncle asks in the next breath.

"Yes, I know it's strange, but it's to find out what the words are without their articles." Barrutia tries to explain the reasoning behind it, but without success. "Fine, fine," Uncle says to him, with scant conviction.

When Uncle is asked for the translation of the word *pulpo* ("octopus") he says *olagarru* and he instantly asks Barrutia, "And in Bermeo, do you know how they say *olagarru* in Bermeo?" *"Amarratza,"* says Barrutia. It sounds for all the world like *hamar hatz* – "ten fingers." "There you go," Uncle declares, *"amarratza,* and that though an octopus has but eight legs."

He goes on, "In Bermeo a lot of words are different. They say *atun txoixak,* 'tuna birds,' and we don't. We call them *martinak* – kingfishers. They're pretty tasty in sauce. You and I would both be much better off if instead of doing this interview we were eating kingfishers."

Kingfishers. Thinking it over, that would have more likely been the actual bird young Bastida saw one thousand five hundred miles from land, a kingfisher, instead of a shag. For of all the birds of the air the kingfisher's the one that travels the farthest from land.

9

LIKE A FLYING FISH

Remembering Uncle, I lost my place in Bastida's diary. I've been reading sentences but don't remember what I've read. I have to go back and start over again.

> June 10
> The steamship's captain seems like good people. He's a clumsy giant. He's sort of pudgy and doesn't have a beard or a mustache and he has white hair. The elevator boy is a musician in the ship's band too, and he plays more musical instruments than the rest of them put together. He plays the drums, the ride cymbals, the crash cymbals, the triangle, the clappers and the castanets. He plays four instruments at the same time. And what's more he was in the African war and he showed me several of the scars they gave him there, and he also has medals. He's the best.

Captain Manuel Aierdi taught classes at the town Fisheries School at the beginning of the nineteen-sixties.

Until then there'd been no school of the kind, people studied navigation in Lekeitio.

When she was already engaged to Dad, a priest named Don Emilio told Mum that she'd be better off going to Gasteiz as a housemaid and marrying an inland boy there, an army man or something. She'd undergo nothing but martyrdom if she married one of the town fishermen. "You'll eat nothing but horse mackerels the whole of your life." When our father heard of this he made Mum a promise, they'd be undergoing no martyrdoms, he'd get his deep-sea captain's certificate.

"Working inshore, you haven't a free moment to study in."

"I'll study over the winter, when the boats are in."

Few in Dad's home crowd had any book learning. With the help of one of them and what he'd learned, the rest ploughed on through those three wintertime months passing exams. The friends would go to the Antzomendi cider house on the Lekeitio road and there's where they'd study together. One fine spring day, Dad called Mum at home, telling her to come down to the square.

"Here you are, what I promised you back then. You'll eat horse mackerels, but only when you want to."

It was his deep-sea captain's certificate.

An older couple stopped me on the street this summer. They introduced themselves. "I'm Overlook Tere," the woman said. "There were three Teres in town and I got stuck with being the Overlook one." I didn't ask her anything more about the nickname, which scenic overlook that might have been. But the nickname struck me as lovely.

Her husband, Tomas Santos, told me he'd worked at sea with our dad and also with our grandfather Liborio. Liborio was said to be a topnotch storyteller, and when Tomas and Tere were little they used to like to go to hear him at his home, on North Street. And he organised the Midsummer's Eve bonfires, too, on North Street, with the help of the children. Of Grandmother Ana, Tomas told me she'd once given him a puppy, and he'd never forget that act of kindness.

Tomas confessed that he'd been carrying around a photograph for me. He'd been wanting to give it to me but never could find me. He showed me the photograph now. It was from the nineteen-sixties, in black and white. In it appear all the men who made it through the fishery-school course. Right in the center the captain, around him twenty-seven students. Dad is in the second row, way young. On either side of him are Tomas and another friend of Dad's, Jon Akarregi.

"You see how many of us were in school back then?" Tomas said to me, pointing at the photograph. "Well, these days there's not one single soul in that school who's studying for captain."

The attachment to the sea has been getting lost in less than no time. Our father's generation spent their first fourteen years hankering after the time they'd go off to sea. When they were younger they'd clamber onto the fishing boats and hide under the nets and, when the craft was at sea, come out of their hiding places.

Our dad, though, didn't want any of us to be seamen. Study and find work ashore, that was our task. And so, of us four siblings I'm the only one who lives in our town. The grandfathers and uncles on both Dad's and Mum's sides were almost all seagoing people. But among us cousins just one chose the sea.

That cousin, Iñaki, is a silent man, like most fishermen, and his gaze is calm, from eyes the colour blue of the ocean in September. He doesn't talk much but when he does pearls come out of his mouth.

As they did when the *Prestige* oil-tanker business took place, in 2002. On its way from Latvia to Gibraltar the vessel went down off the coast of Galicia and released sixty-three thousand tons of oil into the ocean. Straightaway the oil slick spread through the whole of the Cantabrian Sea.

The fishermen decided it was best to clean up the oil out there, before it reached the coast, and the inshore vessels put to sea. One by one they hoisted the tarballs, globs of heavy-crude "galipot," over the side, by hand, as if were bonito. All the same, there's an immense difference between galipot and bonito.

"The smell of that galipot doesn't leave you for days. I don't think anything else on earth has a stink like that. It looked as if the sea was sick, hit by some fatal illness or something," my cousin elaborated, back home.

"One of the crew, Alvaro, a Peruvian guy, told us what he witnessed at home when he was a kid. They lived in the mountains then, in a hut, and he said they had three or four sheep at home. One stormy night, the bleating of a sheep woke him. It was pregnant and couldn't lamb. Only the lamb's feet were out, no way forward, no way back. Pulling at their their feet, Alvaro's father got the lambs out. They were all stillborn. And so, that stink was what the galipot reminded Alvaro of."

The smell of dead lambs in the sea. The thing about the lambs was weird, because when we were little and the wind raised the foam on the waves, they used to tell us that those were the sea sheep.

The sea was calm for the Bastidas when they reached New York.

June 11
The entry into New York was tremendous.
A sunny day, we came in amidst all sizes of

steamships and boats. Some of them were taking passengers up the Hudson River, some were barges carrying trains, warships, cutters etc.

We went to the hotel. The McAlpin Hotel is the world's second biggest hotel, it has 26 stories and cost 13 million dollars. Every day in the hotel they give us a newspaper called *La Prensa* written in Spanish, there are needles with white and black thread, buttons and a telephone. But there aren't any chamberpots, we use the toilet in the bathroom.

The McAlpin Hotel doesn't exist today. At one time it was the most luxurious hotel in New York. But in the nineteen-eighties it went downhill. The city government rented rooms there to put the homeless in. The rooms are apartments now.

While they were staying in New York, Bastida says, they went up in the world's tallest structure, to the fifty-seventh floor of the Woolworth Building. At the time not even the renowned Empire State had been erected. Still and all, skyscraper fever had already begun in New York. The elegant Woolworth Building is an instance. Built in 1911, it's New York's first skyscraper.

In New York the Bastidas will walk across the Brooklyn Bridge from one end to the other. And they'll see Niagara Falls, and the Capitol in Washington. Their destination is Chicago, because the congress is there. On the way they'll see the Armour slaughterhouse, the world's largest. "It's scary, every day they kill 3,000 steers, 24,000 sheep and 48,000 pigs. What's more, one man all by himself finishes off the pigs with an axe."

In Detroit they visited the Ford factory.

June 18

This morning we saw one of the Ford factories, I enjoyed it terrifically, the shops are all gigantic, they told us 65,000 workers usually work there. We didn't see any women workers in the place, but old men yes, doing the easy jobs. Inside the shops there are soft drink and candy stands for the workers, there are showers where they can wash their hair right there. It's a world made for working, and everything is very well prepared, each worker does only one thing and fast and that's why Ford cars are so cheap.

In the hotel, like other places, they take off their hats in the elevators when a lady is

present, but today we saw how everyone kept
his hat on even though a lady was going down,
in point of fact, a lady who was black. Papa
and I uncovered but nobody else did.

A woman stands alongside me and tells me the seat next to
the window is hers. An African American woman in her six-
ties. There was a moment when I thought the seat beside me
was going to stay vacant, and I'd be alone for the length of the
flight. But no. I get up and out into the aisle to let the woman
in. I look at her and find myself smiling. She does the same.

They've closed the doors. The aircraft has started to
move. The flight attendants walk through checking if our
seat belts are fastened. On the little TV in front of me they're
airing the safety measures. Where the life jackets are and so
forth. Very soon, they start showing images from the aircraft's exterior camera. You can see clear as anything how
we're taxiing to the runway. The aircraft pauses at the runway's very tip. They turn off the lights. The flight attendants
take their seats. The great plane gathers power. The camera
is focussed on the runway. You can really see how we pick up
speed. How the plane rises into the air. Clouds. The camera's
switched off.

I remember the people closest to me in those moments
when a plane is taking off.

I know it's childish, but I get scared stiff. And tend to doubt myself.

Have I taken as much care of them as they needed?

Four years or so ago, while I was living in Gasteiz, I was witness to a cruel incident. It was a Saturday night and I'd had something to drink myself by that time. When I was going from one bar to the next, making my way among parked cars, I saw a couple. At the outset I didn't even see them, it was that dark. But the woman's wailing made me notice them. They were in the middle of a fight. Catching sight of me, the man grabbed a set of house keys from the woman and made tracks.

"You'll come back," he kept saying to her threateningly. "You'll come back."

I went up to the woman to see if she was O.K. When she had calmed down a bit she told me he was her husband. And they were about to split up.

I couldn't look her in the face. Her eyes were welling over. I lowered my gaze. At that moment I realised she was barefoot. Her husband had even taken her shoes.

I can't forget that woman's little feet on the tarmac. She was barefoot, as if she'd been condemned to death, like the survivor of a car crash.

"You'll come back," the man had yelled to her, but how was she going to go back barefoot, without any shoes.

That night, I wondered whether I was honest with the people who loved me. If my life was heading downhill, with me totally unaware.

They turn on the lights. The fasten-seat-belts sign goes off. The plane settles into its outbound flight path, making for the Atlantic crossing. I've got just a few pages to go before I finish the diary.

June 30–July 6

I've seen a lot of flying fish, they're slightly bigger than sardines. Sometimes one comes out of the water, goes flying and then dives back in again. Other times a school of them come shooting out, and after they fly they dive back in all together. Their flights aren't normally longer than 100 metres, almost always in a straight line and a few times making a turn. We also saw a whale off the port side, the parts that broke the water must have been 10 or 12 metres apart.

As we get closer to Europe we're seeing a lot of steamships. We've overtaken two ocean liners. One was huge.

That's how young Bastida's journal ends. I can see the red evening sun out the small cabin window. The wing of the aircraft sparkles, like those flying fish.

10

DUBLIN

Distance to Destination: 3,169 miles
Time to destination: 6:06 hours
Local Time: 01:08 PM
Ground Speed: 544 mph
Altitude: 35,000
Outside air temperature: -72° F
St. Kilda, Londonderry, Donegal

"Excuse me prying, but what's that you've been reading?" the woman beside me suddenly asks.

"It's a diary."

"It looks to be from a while back."

"It sure is. A fourteen-year-old boy wrote it in 1926."

"Your grandfather?"

"No, the son of an architect back then. He went on a trip with his father from Europe to the United States."

"You don't say. And how did it come into your hands?"

"I'm a writer and doing research for a novel."

"A writer? Well, hey, I work surrounded by books. I'm a New York Public Library employee. Pardon me, I haven't introduced myself. Renata Thomas. All right, Renata Violet

Thomas. They gave me that 'Violet' for my grandmother. Greatest lady in the state of South Carolina."

"Kirmen Uribe. I'm glad to meet you."

"That name, is it in your language?"

"In Basque."

"Is that so? That's the first thing I've ever heard in Basque. Interesting . . . And what's taking you to New York?"

"I've got a friend who's a professor at New York University, Mark Rudman. He teaches poetry classes and invited me to give a little talk."

"On poetry? I'm not a good reader of poetry at all. . . ."

"It's not just about poetry. I've given it the title 'The Gravestones in Käsmu.' Käsmu is a small village in Estonia, beside the Baltic. Writers from seven of Europe's languages got together there, and I was one of them."

"How interesting."

"And you, what brought you to Europe?"

"My daddy did. He was a G.I. in Italy during the Second World War, and I wanted to see the places he'd been in. To be in those places whose names my sister and I kept hearing when we were little. I spent some time in the cemetery at Certosa, six miles or so from Florence. Four thousand five hundred American soldiers are buried there. It's terrifying, tremendous!"

"Our grandmother often used to talk to us about the Italian soldiers. From the six months the front was in our town during the Spanish Civil War. The men in town escaped in their boats for the Bilbao area, for fear of forced conscription or worse. Grandma was left alone. The thing is, the Italian soldiers did enter the town and were going after the women there."

"After your grandma too?"

"The ones who could, yeah. Grandma had quite a temper and would wave an axe out the window at them."

"I like your grandma."

"Anyhow, there were also people who had a bad time. There's one song that's an example of that."

"And the song goes how?"

> "Turubi brings, Turubi brings
> a teensy tiny baby
> and black as ink, and black as ink
> the teensy Eye-talian baby."

"Man, it must have been rough on that woman."

"You know how it is. Things in small towns."

While he was in the process of making the Logroño seminary mural, Arteta gave his sketches to Bastida. What he drew first on paper and then would paint in the mural, what after being made in small had to be made in large. Bastida was left in possession of many of those sketches.

Bastida was in the habit of sending some of the pieces Arteta painted to the socialist politician Indalecio Prieto. They'd be things like images of the Virgin Mother – the religious stuff. He knew that Prieto was an agnostic and didn't believe in such things, but that's precisely why he kept on sending them. "Since I know how much pleasure you take in Arteta's work, I'm sending you this picture for your enjoyment." That kind of phrasing was regular in his letters.

It was a game between them, the one a monarchist and the other a socialist. Prieto was hugely amused by Bastida's lifelong attempt to turn him into a believer. He truly admired the attempt, and especially, he admired Bastida. They'd met each other in Bilbao's city council in 1916, when Prieto came in as a councillor. They got to be friends and worked on a great number of projects together.

When Prieto went into exile for the first time, as a result of the 1917 general strike, it seems Ricardo Bastida put him in touch with a fisherman from Ondarroa. Who would get him out of Bilbao and take him to Saint-Jean de Luz.

Nonetheless, the episode that was supposedly going to be heroic turned into something funny. Out of Bilbao they got, but late. Because they'd arranged a meeting and the fisherman did not show up. The next time he did, though then too, as Prieto tells in his memoirs, late.

Sebastian Bakeriza, Prieto's hypothetical savior, turned up in Bilbao with a small launch. He had his father with him, an aged fisherman, as his only crew and deckhand. Bakeriza's father spoke only Basque, and even Bakeriza himself spoke Spanish with great difficulty. Prieto, for his part, didn't know a word of Basque.

They had Prieto get into the storeroom in the fishhold, and there he stayed among the nets for a long, long time. Done in, his back aching, Prieto opened the fishhold hatch and stuck his head out. In the distance, he saw a lighthouse. Since they'd been underway for hours and hours, he asked the fishermen if that off there was Matxitxa light. Sebastian answered no, it was Galea. "Galea light – we 're not out of the Bilbao estuary yet!"

The boat's engine was flooded and they'd been adrift in the Ibaizabal's estuary, unable to get out. Worst of all, though, was that they couldn't go on like that. They needed to put in somewhere, no matter how, and leave the escape for another time.

The best plan would be to go back up into Bilbao, Prieto told the Bakerizas. Sebastian told him he didn't know the port of Bilbao and didn't know how to put in. And so, with Prieto himself as navigator they got up to somewhere in the city near

Mazarredo and that's where Prieto leapt off, across from the *El Liberal* newspaper building. Leapt in the larger matter as well, since the newspaper building faced a police station.

In the end Prieto made his escape to Saint-Jean on a freighter. But during that four-hour-long adventure Prieto and Bakeriza became fast friends.

Such fast friends that a few years later Bakeriza himself went to Madrid along with the mayor of Ondarroa, to see Prieto when he'd been appointed minister of Urban Planning. They wanted to ask the new minister to renovate the port facilities in town, because of that dangerous stretch at the entry to the fish docks.

Bakeriza and the mayor reach the minister's door. They tell the gatekeeper they have to see Prieto. But the gatekeeper, taking in what they look like, doesn't believe them and turns them away. Bakeriza says he won't leave until he's seen Prieto, the minister is his close friend. The gatekeeper: gentlemen, I insist, please get out of here. Bakeriza: don't even think it. Some pushing and shoving, some shouting. Prieto himself comes out of his office asking what all the ruckus is. He recognises Bakeriza. He has them come into the office. "They're old, old friends."

In 1932 the plan for the new port was approved, a few days after Bakeriza's visit. That's one time when Bakeriza really hit upon the right strategy.

In the port construction, anyhow, Juan Jose Mancisdor played a decisive role. When I Googled the words "Prieto + Ondarroa," a number of site links turned up. The eighth was a portal called Diving XXI. There I found an article about the scuba diver Mancisdor.

Born in Mutriku in 1872, Juan Jose Mancisdor settled in Ondarroa. He was the pioneer among scuba divers. Before long his fame in diving circles had spread all along the Cantabrian coast. Because of this, when Alfonso XIII's launch got caught on a snag, Mancisdor was the one they called on to free up the vessel. The propeller was snagged on some kind of line and the *Giralda* couldn't move, no way forward, no way back. When he saw the tangle, Mancisdor asked if he could possibly use dynamite. The captain said yes, to do whatever he needed to. No sooner said than done.

Once he'd got it free the captain asked him how much it was. "Nothing at all. I don't want cash for something like this" was Mancisdor's reply. When the king learned that Mancisdor didn't want to charge any money, he asked if there was any other way he might be repaid for the favor he'd done.

"Let me take what I want from the floor of the bay of La Concha," Mancisdor answered without thinking twice. And so he took from those waters anchors, old crates, coins and other objects.

It was Indalecio Prieto who brought Ondarroa's new port project into being. He got the project started, but when Mancisdor set eyes on the plans he said he could do the work a lot more cheaply, and sooner, if they dried up the whole bay, putting down cofferdams, instead of being in construction for years. He knew the seabed of the port like the back of his hand.

The Urban Planning minister took his opinions into account. They drained the entire bay, dried out the bay floor and made the new seawalls just as if they were working on shore.

According to the Google article, Mancisdor died right in Ondarroa, while he was helping to raise a crane that had collapsed, in 1937.

"Do you know who I am?" a woman asked me as she held on to my cheeks with both hands. We were in a restaurant in town and I was on my way to the bathroom. In the spring of this year. The woman came up to me as I was passing the bar. Her eyes were welling over, as bright as could be. "I'm Pepper Antigua. I'm Miel's wife," she said. "Your mother told me you wanted to spend some time with me gathering stories for a book. Your dad and my husband were among the first to go off to Rockall. Whenever you want, come by the house and we'll visit." She was still holding on to my hands.

She was named Antigua, just like our mother. Everyone in her family was called Pepper.

"I'm Miel's wife," she said and walked away. "I'm Miel's wife," twice.

I was moved by how proudly this widowed woman said whose wife she'd been; despite the many years since her husband had died, she spoke of him with such pride. She was still his wife.

Miel Gallastegi was machinist on the *Toki-Argia* for many years. Since our dad was captain, more than once he'd asked Miel for advice. Which route they'd take, where they'd set the net.

The relationship between captain and machinist on a boat is tight. That's how it has to be. At one time it was carpenters on fishing boats. That in the era of sailing ships. It was essential to have carpenters on the crew. If there was some breakup, if the mast went awry, if there was no carpenter aboard the vessel was sunk. And so there were usually three or four carpenters on sailing ships. And there was always a contest between the captain and the head carpenter. The captain tended to want to go faster, to put the mast's resistance to the test. The carpenter, though, tended to want to go slower, wanted to take good care of the boat, to get back into port in one piece. I've often thought we all have the same contest going on in us. That we have a captain who wants to take risks and then the carpenter, who'd prefer to maintain the reservoirs, to play it safe.

Later it was the machinists who took the carpenters' place. And the contest has gone on, exactly the same, down to the present day. The machinist wants to take care of the machine, so it won't overheat. The captain wants to navigate using the whole of the machine.

Miel used to paint. Once he promised our dad that he'd paint a picture of the incident in which British soldiers detained the *Toki-Argia* and took her under guard to Stornoway port, and would make him a present of the picture.

In 1998 Miel gave the picture to our father at last. With the title "The Capture of the *Toki-Argia*." In the picture is the boat itself. A black trawler, flying on its smokestack the Larrauri Bros. company flag, in red and black. Beside the trawler is the coast-guard cutter. *Jura* is its name. An inflatable tender is leaving the cutter and heading for the *Toki-Argia*. On the fishing boat meanwhile, a netful of fish is rising over the side.

"That was a glorious haul," Miel said to Dad when he gave him the picture. At the bottom there's a date: Rockall, May 22, 1982. That was the day they took the boat under guard.

11

THE GRAVESTONES IN KÄSMU

That's where I heard the cuckoo the last time. I haven't
heard one since.

It was in the forests of Estonia, in May 2004. We took a
walk in the mountains, a group of writers, and we heard it
right there, in the heart of that dark forest, singing.

We were taking part in a writers' retreat in a small village named Käsmu. Käsmu is a tiny village by the shore of
the Baltic; it's truly tiny, it can't have more than a dozen
houses, and some three hundred inhabitants.

After our walk in the mountains they invited us to eat supper in a building beside the beach. We had to eat supper by
daylight, since it was the end of May and at that time of year
in Estonia they've got only three or four hours of nighttime.

That house beside the beach was lovely. It must've been
the largest house in the village. Wide stretches of wood-
framed windows. The doors and the window frames in
white. The walls light blue. In the front dooryard a flower
garden, well kept, and on the beach the hull of an old dory.

The building had been the coast guard's in Soviet times.
And still earlier, a school for sea captains. Now several married couples lived there. Inside they'd set up a museum-like

space. With old sea gear and navigation equipment. There were old photographs, too, hanging on the walls. In these photos were the captains, as elegant as anything, in their uniforms.

As I looked at the portraits close-up I took it in just as the head of the household murmured by my ear, "They're Germans." He went on, "In the days of the czars most Russian naval officers were German." A lot of state posts were in German hands at the time, and most scientists, too, came from Germany. "That until the revolution arrived," he explained, with a sad look.

The man talked to me of the revolution and the captains on our way to the village graveyard. "Outsiders think there was a socialist revolution in our village as well. But it was actually nothing but the Russians' conquest." Dissidents had gone to take refuge in those dark forests round about. "Some of them spent years and years living in the forests. Never coming out." Then he plucked a sprig of greenery from the roadside and gave it to me to try, saying it was edible.

The small Käsmu graveyard is one of those graveyards that turn up on seacoasts. Its church is wooden, painted white, and the gravestones are inside a wooden fence. The most tremendous discovery I made in the days I spent in Käsmu I made in that very graveyard. There I happened on something I had never seen before.

The man told us to look at the names on the gravestones. On most of them two given names appeared, with only one surname. On the gravestones were the names of married couples:

Hasso Liive (1935–1999)
Ilvi Liive (1938–   )

I wrote it down in my notebook just like that.

The strange thing wasn't for the husband and wife to be together. What was unusual was this: that when one died, they wrote on the stone the name of the other as well. And the one who was still alive, each time they went to visit the cemetery, would see their own name etched on that gravestone. Alive and written-down. They knew where their days would end, and at whose side, because that was the way it was, by fate.

The Estonians believe that if people are buried together they'll be together in the next life too. That's how the coast-guard–house fellow told it to us. While we were there, the Estonian poet Doris Kaveva told us an old story. She'd been reminded of it by the whole affair of the gravestones.

It was the story of the grandmother of a friend of hers. How when she was young, she and a boy had fallen in love. They did fall in love, yes, but life didn't want them to be together. One had to go off one way and the other another. The boy left the village and the girl stayed behind. And so it was, they met other people and even married them and had children. But in their secret hearts their love for each other continued, alive as could be. And that love lasted, year in and year out. One day, the man did return to the village. And in that small village they tended to meet up with each other, but each one's life was even then running on its different path. It was too late for them to get together. They kept on in that way until one of them, the man, died.

They'd already made a promise to each other, that though they wouldn't be together in life, they would after death, and forever. At long last the woman managed to get her own burial plot placed next to that of the man. Their people would've buried them each with their own spouse but instead they would be buried beside each other, the two abreast, close enough to take the other's hand.

Doris found that woman's love story sublime. The woman was courageous, it seemed to her, and love in the end had carried the day. Somehow they would indeed at long last manage to be together.

The Welsh writer Mererid Puw Davies didn't agree. Mererid, a poet twenty years younger than Doris, didn't want to accept the fate of it. And even less the sentence their society had passed on the two of them.

The whole of it had struck Mererid as horrible. Horrible on the one hand to write both names on the gravestone. And horrible, on the other, what had happened to that grandmother.

"Is there really no way to change course while we're still alive? Do we have no chance at all to begin another life?"

I ate supper sitting next to Mererid. We were directly across the table from the Scots poet Alan Jamieson. Alan's from the Shetland Islands but lives in Edinburgh now. I told Alan about the fishermen who worked off Rockall, and how Dad often mentioned the name of one port: Stornoway.

"You've got more than one fine writer in Stornoway, Kevin MacNeil's amongst them. I think I've one of the few copies of his book of poems in my room."

Before supper each poet had had to read a poem and that's what we did, each in our own language. Doris went last:

> *Naine on vesi – selge,*
> *Puhas ja igavene.*
>
> *Mehed on maitseained*
> *sajandi supi sees.*
>
> [Woman is water,
> Water that's clean and eternal.

Men are but salt and pepper
in this night's soup.]

After supper Mererid took up the subject of the gravestones again: why the penchant for always hoeing the same
row, why believe things can only be done in a single way. The
same in literature. Our small cultures had to get renewed.
The ways of doing things renewed. To adapt to the times. The
medium has changed. Nowadays it's not just books. Right
there, you've got your new technologies. And who's on the
receiving end has changed too. No one was writing solely
for the fellow members of their own community now. The
world's smaller. The people of Tallin would be listening to
us on Saturday. And just a few years ago that was impossible.

"Anyhow," she said, "I suspect we don't believe in ourselves as much as we need to. Our energies are too scattered." She paused. "Let me tell you what happened during
the war in the Falklands. The Argentines took the Malvinas
and the navy of the United Kingdom went off to liberate the
Falklands. It so happened there were Welsh-speaking people
in both navies. On one side were people who had gone out
from Wales, under the Queen. And on the other side were
the Welsh who were defending the dictator of Argentina. For
a great many Welsh people live in Argentina, in some parts
only Welsh is spoken, in Patagonia and thereabouts. They

fought against each other. In the trenches on both sides you heard the same language. And so, it does seem we're still stuck in that war."

An older man who'd eaten supper with us broke in on Mererid's observations, he'd taken up a spoon and was clinking it on a drinking glass, asking for silence. He introduced himself: "Good evening, I'm Fred, a naturalist, and I'd like you all to hear something," he said, and put a CD in the sound system. It was the songs of birds, cheep-cheep-cheeping, those birds.

"How many kinds of bird do you think are in there?" he asked us afterward. "One or two," someone answered, "Three or four," said someone else. "Well, no," Fred said. "There are twenty kinds of song there, twenty different birds all singing at once." And he likened the birds' performance to the reading we'd just done. "Listening to you, it sounded as if you were birds singing. I've been listening to birds in the forests here for forty years. I haven't understood their song but I knew what they were feeling. I knew when they were cold or hungry, I knew when they were stricken with some disease, or in love. And myself, though I didn't understand you word for word, I know what you were meaning to tell me. But nevertheless, you yourselves, you've been incapable of distinguishing the songs of a couple of birds. You heard only the ones on top, only the loudest."

I went outside. It was the small hours of the morning but the sky still hadn't gone completely dark. You could see a reddish line on the horizon. The eye of a child who doesn't want to go to sleep. Fred came up beside me and he, too, stood and examined the sky. Without taking my eyes off the horizon I told him that the thing about the birds had been beautiful. It had taught us a lesson.

"That was no lesson," said the naturalist. "Half the world hasn't heard word one about the other half." He was still gazing out at the border of the sky. "I've spent forty years of my life listening to birds, I know everything you need to know about birdsong. But I'm incapable of singing myself. I've never in my life written a single line. I myself wanted to be a poet, but I've never been able to write a word, fear got the better of me."

I heard the cuckoo the last time in the forests of Estonia. It's our old folk belief that if you have coins in your pocket when you hear the first cuckoo, you'll have money in your pocket the whole coming year.

I didn't have a single coin in my pocket at the time, but I did come home with my trousers full of poems.

12

A BIRD IN THROUGH THE WINDOW

When I'd finished writing the talk I sent it to Nerea by email. I was happy with it but I wanted to know her opinion. She answered me right back:

From: Nerea Arrieta,
    nerearrieta@euskalnet.net
To: Kirmen Uribe, kirmen@gmail.com
Date: 07-27-2008
Subject: cuckoo congress

So you had a cuckoo congress in Estonia, did you? That's what our grandmother used to say, you know, for when three or four friends are talking in whispers. Your ending turned out poetical. I'm going to tell you a more realistic story. Once, two friends were hiking up in the mountains and they heard the cuckoo singing. Since both of the two had coins in their pockets, they immediately took to disputing. "It sang to me," said the one. "Not on your life," said the other, "that cuckoo was singing to me." Since they weren't getting anywhere near a solution, they decided to go to a notary to clear things up. The notary told them that before doing anything they'd have to lay out five pesetas apiece, then they'd get down to business. Once they'd paid up they told the notary what had happened and asked him who it was the cuckoo'd sung to.

"Who did the cuckoo sing to?" the notary said. "Not to you, and not to you either. Today the cuckoo sang to me!"

That one is our grandma's too.
I'm swamped right now. I'll call you.
Kisses!

"Pasta or meat," the flight attendant asks us. "L. Thompson," it says on her lapel. She's here with the meal cart handing out supper trays. Both Renata and I pick pasta. To drink, red wine. *Danke. Bitte.*

"You haven't told me what that novel of yours is about," Renata asks me as she frees her tableware from its plastic pouch.

"It's a long story."

"Hmm. That's not good. You know a good novelist has to know how to define his novel in three or four lines."

"I'll try."

"Out with it."

"My first idea was to write about my grandfather's boat. And simultaneously, about a way of life that's in the process of getting lost. The way of life that's bound up with the sea. The name of the boat is suggestive too. *Dos Amigos.* Two friends."

"Really nice."

"I've always wanted to know why our granddad named his boat that. I've been looking into who that alleged friend of his was, but nothing's come clear."

"*Dos Amigos,* like the slave ship?"

"Slave ship?"

"You don't know it? It's a slave ship, important in the history of the United States. Moreover, the story's got its sum and substance. A politician named Douglas Wilder, once governor of Virginia and then the mayor of Richmond, put in for a two-billion-dollar cash grant from Washington to build a U.S. National Slavery Museum. The building itself was going to be meaningful, take its inspiration from the pyramid at the Louvre. The most striking thing about it was going to be a life-size replica of the slave ship *Dos Amigos.* So people could see how the slaves made the crossing, in what kind of conditions, one on top of the other in one small space."

"That's quite a coincidence, its having the same name as our grandfather's boat."

"What happened with the *Dos Amigos* was brutal."

"Tell me."

"In the fall of 1830 the British naval barque *Black Joke* caught up with the slave ship *Dos Amigos* off the island of Fernando Pó. According to what the *Black Joke*'s captain William Ramsey wrote, that ship was carrying more than five hundred slaves to Cuba. A gentleman named Muxika was the captain of the *Dos Amigos*."

"Excuse me, but what name did you say?"

"M-u-x-i-k-a."

"It sounds like a Basque name."

"It could be, since it was a Cuban ship."

"But anyway, sorry, please go on."

"O.K. That Muxika saw HMS *Black Joke* coming up on them from behind, and he knew that sooner or later she'd catch up with them. To keep from getting caught, Muxika decided they'd have to lose some ballast. And so, they threw more than five hundred slaves into the water, near the island so they'd swim there, and tossed out bundles of food for them, too, so they'd last a few days. Muxika's intention was plain: without the ballast he'd increase his ship's speed and put one over on the *Black Joke*. Once they'd lost the trail he'd go back to Fernando Pó, pick up the slaves and take them on to Cuba."

"As if they were merchandise."

"That's just what they were, for them. But let me finish. The *Black Joke* was too quick and caught the *Dos Amigos* as she was putting out from the island. The officials took them under guard but it was impossible to take five hundred and sixty-three slaves aboard the *Black Joke*."

"Don't tell me."

"From that time on, they turned the *Dos Amigos* into a slave catcher. They changed the old name and rechristened her the *Fair Rosamond* and under that name she went about her new mission."

"And what happened to the five hundred and sixty-three Africans?"

"Nobody went back to look for those defenceless Africans who got left on the island. What's worst of all is that this U.S. National Slavery Museum project is as sunk in oblivion as those five hundred and sixty-three Africans. Even now there's no building plan."

"You know a lot about this subject."

"It's my job. I work at the Schomburg Center for Research in Black Culture, in Harlem. Also I've always been interested in researching my roots."

"I was in Harlem once, in May of this year. I went to the assembly of the American Academy of Arts and Letters."

"Not bad."

"Yeah, the writer Elizabeth Macklin, who translated my book, invited me to go with her. You won't believe this. I showed up wearing a dress suit, there at the door of the Academy. But then I realised I wasn't seeing much movement anywhere around. At some point I asked a few Hispanics who were unloading canapés what time the gathering was. It wasn't for another whole hour!"

"And what did you do for that whole hour?"

"All I could think of was, there I was in the middle of Harlem wearing a Gucci suit. I wanted to go get a cup of coffee but I didn't dare go into any of the places around there dressed like that. I was afraid."

"Afraid?"

"Yes, and so there I stood without moving more than ten feet from the main entrance for the whole hour. The best part is, when the gala was all over I wanted to go to the restaurant Soto for dinner with Elizabeth and we didn't know the address. Elizabeth said: we'll Google it there in that cybercafé across the street. Will you believe me if I tell you we went into that cybercafé and no one even glanced at me?"

"Of course they didn't. Preconceptions are powerful. All the same, some places it's better not to venture."

"Do you know, in our town we never saw any black people until just a little while ago?"

"Is that so?"

"Yes, but look at how things are. Now black people are five per cent of the population in a town of nine thousand inhabitants. None of us kids in town wanted to go to sea and now they're the fishermen."

"How did that happen?"

"In 2001 the boat owners sent out a recruiting call for fishermen and they came from Senegal. There's a big sea-going tradition there. Especially in Dakar. Most of them are of the Serer Nominka tribe. The meaning of the name is nice. 'Sea folk.'"

"'Sea folk.' I think they've been having you on. You writers see everything so nice. Now, wait, I'm joshing you. It could be that that's the case. The Serer tribe is a nomadic tribe, that's what Senghor said anyhow. And the sea-folk business could come from that."

"But the Ondarroa fishermen's itinerary bears some kind of resemblance to the Cuban *Dos Amigos'*. The first of them came with work contracts, but then others came after crossing in makeshift boats from Mauritania to the Canary Islands. Over forty people in a little boat. With luck the journey can last them twelve hours. Depart at seven in the evening and arrive at seven in the morning. But some ended up adrift at sea for days."

I'm remembering Uncle Boni. He used to watch TV from his bed, though most of the time largely tuning it out. This one time, though, he was watching intently. On TV they were showing the corpses of several dead immigrants at the Strait of Gibraltar. His mood darkened at the sight of them. I asked him what was wrong and he commanded me to look at the TV set. "There's a deal of wind in that strait," he said then, "nearly no waves at all but the wind is fearsome. That's why it's in your interest not to make straight across, your boat's always got to run inshore, alee of the shore. The boat's got to come about in a wide turn to cross the strait, so the wind doesn't take her under. And as if that weren't enough, the big freighters tear through there at full steam and it's in your interest to take good care not to run into one of those."

He was sick but was still eminently clear on all the things that he'd learned at sea. "What's happening to those poor souls is a true bitch. Because of the wind their boat's filling up with water, but don't imagine they're awash on account of some big wave, no sir. It's spatter by spatter, spray filling the boat with water, bit by bit. They try to bail the water out in buckets, but most times nothing they do is any use."

When the segment on the drowned immigrants was over he turned off the TV and sat looking at the wall, as if he were trying to recall something that had happened years before. "The Basques, too, we've been in straits as dire as that. In the postwar the seaway from Ondarroa to Angelu was as rough a crossing as the Strait of Gibraltar. Loads of people fled by sea up to Labourd and thereabouts. In small boats too. A fellow who'd worked on our launch, Fidel, told me what I'll tell you now. When we were fishing the shallows off the Landes we took the launch in to Bordeaux. Fidel came up and asked if I'd go for a walk with him. We left the rest of the crew in the port and Fidel took me to a graveyard that was somewhere up around there. That cemetery was huge, bristling with crosses. Fidel had fought in that very place. Matter of fact, he was one of those who'd escaped north across the border. But no sooner did the man reach Labourd than the Second World War caught him. He enlisted against the Nazis. They say the battle of Bordeaux was the hardest. Bits of flesh kept flying into his face. In that field with those white crosses. In that field where the sun was shining."

I'm not capable of keeping a daily diary. I jot things down in notebooks, things that come into my mind, what I'm reading and other kinds of information, errands maybe, or telephone numbers. All of those things are my daily diary.

After living in Bilbao and Gasteiz, I moved back to my hometown in the fall of 2005. From the time I moved out to go to college until then I'd been back only every once in a while.

On July 28, 2005, this is what I wrote in my notebook:

> I got to Ondarroa on Sunday. It calms me down to be here. I've been wanting to keep on with the novel project but I can't. In the P.M. when I was messing with a very few lines of it a bird flew into the room. It was so fragile, fluttering around and around smashing into the walls. I opened the window wide and it got itself out. The way it looks to me, I'm just as mixed up as that bird, as disoriented.
>
> Noontime today they told me this one episode. During the Republic there was supposedly a socialist in town called Meabe. The man was a bird fancier, tamed and trained songbirds. He had who knows how many songbirds.
>
> Once, in the war, a bomb destroyed his house and all the birds flew out. By then, Meabe had got away from town. People talked about it like a magical thing, after a severe

explosion hundreds of songbirds flying free in the streets. After a brutal event like that, after the fear, after the destruction, for a moment joy had taken over those streets.

The birds belonged to Santi Meabe, from Bilbao originally. He was among the finest of bird trainers. Even before the birds got free on their own with the bomb, Meabe himself had set the birds loose, in 1935 when he returned from prison, opening the cages with a "Take off, guys, you're free too." In Meabe's opinion, birds trained on the coast were best of all, because they learned how to sing against the sea. Even when he was living in Normandy, in charge of caring for the Republican refugees there, he kept on training birds and lulled the hardships of the war for himself with their song.

Santi Meabe was the brother of the socialist leader Tomas Meabe. Love brought Santi to Ondarroa. He fell in love with Salbadora Goitia and married her. They had a clothing store, below the church in town.

People used to call Santi Meabe "Fallen Leaf," making fun of him. And in point of fact he had a strange political evolution. At the outset he was a nationalist, a member of the Basque Nationalist Party, in keeping with the tradition he'd gotten at home. As the years went by, he'd been one of the founders of Basque Nationalist Action in a laic schism, and ended up at last in the socialist party. The fallen-leaf business came out of all that.

During the war he directed the defence of the Republic in Ondarroa's Lea-Artibai district. One of the first decisions he made was to tear down the bridges. And so it came to pass that they demolished Ondarroa's old bridge with dynamite, so the Francoists couldn't cross it. That old bridge the painters had so often painted, which had been the symbol of an old world, was brought down by the war.

The bridge was destroyed twice. The first time was then, during the war. The second time, it was washed away in a flood, on the very day the architect Ricardo Bastida died.

THE BOATS THAT COME INTO PORT

Ricardo Bastida died on November 15, 1953. Bastida had learned that Indalecio Prieto was feeling unwell and wanted to pay him a visit in Mexico, since Arteta, too, was living in exile there. But on the plane he fell ill. Just as soon as he reached the Mexico City airport he got a flight back home.

It wasn't the first occasion Bastida had gone to visit Prieto in exile. In 1948 they spent time together in Saint-Jean de Luz. They talked over all the old perennial subjects. Especially the years of their Bilbao childhood. The Carnaval big-heads and Carnaval giants, that figure they call Gargantua and more. The huge papier-mâché giant Gargantua who swallows the children. Prieto had enjoyed climbing into Gargantua's mouth over and over, and sliding down and out his ass. Bastida, however, had not. It made him self-conscious to do such a thing in front of people.

They wrangled, and how, over religion. They bemoaned the urban-planning projects that they'd dreamt up together for the city during the Republic. How the war caused all of it to be abandoned. That great train station, especially. Prieto would tell people of Bastida's utter discouragement at the effects of the war.

The Francoist uprising caught Bastida in Ondarroa. It was July and he was on vacation there. He immediately felt trapped between the two sides. For some people he was too conservative, for others the friend of socialists.

The architect's son died at the front, on September 15, 1937. The Nationals had conscripted him. Young Ricardo Bastida was only twenty-five when they killed him. Eleven years earlier he'd written that candid, plainspoken journal on his trip to the United States with his father. That same diary I've just finished reading on this plane. When he took that trip the world was wide open and full of attractions. It was vicious during the war, though.

"And now," Bastida once wrote to Prieto, "they're asking the families of National Front civil-war dead if we're willing for our relatives' bodies to be buried in the Valley of the Fallen, down in Madrid. Lord God forgive the people who go around saying things like that! All of the soldiers are the fallen. Death made a brother of every one of the soldiers and, in consequence, they are all brothers together."

His relationship with Prieto created big headaches for Bastida. Despite Bastida's being the architect of the bishop's residence and a member of the Catholic Action association, the Francoists denounced him and he lost his position and his salary in the Bilbao municipal government. What's more, he was in danger of going to jail.

Once, Bastida met up on the street with the man who'd brought the denunciation against him. Bastida noticed that the fellow became nervous as he approached him. The architect said to him no more than these two sentences: "I've just come to tell you that I forgive you. Forgiveness is going to be my revenge."

I don't know if Miel Gallastegi, the *Toki-Argia*'s machinist, was able to forgive the suffering they caused him during the war. If at some point he achieved peace inside himself. I'd say so, having known him. I'd say he overcame the grief and the hatred at the very least. Going by what people have told me, at least.

My memories of when the *Toki-Argia* would come in to port are hazy. I can say, beyond the shadow of a doubt, that a flock of people would gather down there, the women would stand around with us children waiting for the boat to come in. Fishermen might have left a pregnant wife when they put out to sea and find her with a baby carriage when they got back in. "Talking's one thing and living's another," our mother used to say to us. "We didn't experience too many things with our husbands in our daily lives, since one would be at sea and the other on shore. We'd tell each other things. But they were things that had already happened."

We children, too, spent little time with our dad. Sometimes Mum would tell him to give us a talking-to if we'd misbehaved. "Go to the kids' room and give them a talking-to." But when Dad came into the room he'd sit down on the edge of the bed and there he'd sit, looking at us, silent as could be.

The boat would get in and the seamen begin coming off with their big blue duffel bags. I remember Miel the machinist very well. How could a kid forget him, since he disembarked carrying tiny whittled ships in his hand. Because the hours in the engine room were long, Miel made little reproductions of ships. If the sea was good, that is.

There's a long tradition of model-ship makers in our town. The oldest of the models is a frigate that hangs in the Antigua hermitage, from the nineteenth century. Jose Mauri y Kaiser is said to have made it, as an ex-voto for the church.

Fernando Iramategi restored that Antigua ship in the nineteen-fifties. Fernando Iramategi's fame had spread beyond the town, especially among the summer people. Ricardo Bastida and Jose Maria Oriol y Urquijo deeply admired his work. Especially Oriol. Oriol once saw a fine ship in a display window. It, too, was Iramategi's, there could be no doubt of that. Oriol thought it was the most spectacular ship he'd ever seen. A masterwork. It was tremendous how much care had been taken over every detail. Iramategi had reached the height of his art.

That sailing ship so struck Oriol that he asked the artisan to sell it, please sell it, because he wanted it for his very own. He'd give Iramategi whatever amount of money he wanted for that work. It didn't matter a damn to him how many thousands of hours he'd put into making it. He'd pay him for every one, and pay well too. But Iramategi said no. The artisan was a serious man, he'd given his word and couldn't do such a thing. And he told Oriol this: the ship was destined for a raffle and there was no going back on it. If Oriol liked, he could buy a raffle ticket and, beyond that, wait to see what luck or God above decided.

Jose Maria Oriol was left uneasy by his conversation with Iramategi. And each time he saw that glorious ship, he got butterflies in his stomach. He wanted it for his own no matter what it took. He couldn't imagine that ship alighting in someone else's house simply because somebody besides himself had better luck on raffle day. Oriol was in no way a partisan of leaving things to luck. Not in his private life, and not in business matters either. Oriol was a partisan of decisiveness, he was one of those people who believe in striking while the iron is hot.

At length raffle day arrived. Oriol had, one by one, bought up every single raffle ticket, he got his hands on all the paper slips first. And thus he became the owner of that fine ship of Iramategi the master. Some things simply must not be left to fate, no matter what.

In town they used to call Miel Gallastegi "Madrileño Miel." The nickname was appropriate, since in fact he'd been born in Madrid, though his father was an Ondarroan born and bred. Apparently, Miel's father wasn't a seaman born and bred, since he tended to get seasick, and his family sent him inland to Eibar to work at the Star arms factory.

There they saw that the boy had talents and they sent him on to the headquarters of the National Mint in Madrid, to design coins and paper money there. In Madrid he got married, and also got a good position, for in the summer they'd come up to Urberuaga, to the mineral springs there, the way the summer people did. Miel when he was little never wanted to come up here. He didn't want to leave Madrid, he was studying at the Free Institution for Education and he would far rather have gone to the summer camp the Institution had set up, over in Cantabria.

He didn't want to have anything to do with that little town of his father's.

When the war came, though, things went askew. The house the Gallastegis had in Argüelles was destroyed in a Francoist bombardment. Miel's grandparents fled from Madrid to Alicante and they died there. His mother couldn't bear the death of her mother and she too died, of grief, Miel said.

When Madrid fell to the Francoists they took Miel's father prisoner. A bit later, they selected him to do mechanic's work, and that job gave him a chance to spend a few hours outside the prison. That saved his life. Unfortunately, once the war was over things changed down to the ground. The repression intensified. They ordered reprisal shootings. That was precisely how they killed Miel's father.

Just in case, his father had given Miel a slip of paper with some addresses on it. He suspected that they were going to kill him sooner or later, one way or another. He told Miel that if anything happened to him, to go to one of those addresses and they would welcome him in. All the addresses were in Ondarroa.

At age fifteen, with neither shelter, shade, nor home, Miel came by train from Madrid to San Sebastian. He got the coast train to Deba. In Deba he saw there was a bus going to Ondarroa and showed his slip of paper to the driver, asking if he happened to know anyone on the list. The bus driver took Miel to 12 North Street, and there the Pepper family took him in. The name of the street had been changed by that time, it would be Commandant Velarde Street for the future. The Pepper family took Miel into their home, this teenage boy they'd never seen before.

Liborio and Ana lived in the same building, in the basement apartment.

Miel told all these things to one of his small grandchildren and that grandchild recorded them for a school project not long before Miel died. When I went to visit Pepper Antigua she lent me the recording, saying, "Right here is Miel's whole essence."

The CD is intensely alive. For one thing Miel's sense of humor, and for another the child's laughter. At one thing that happened to them during the Second World War, for instance. Apparently they were coasting off France in the mid-nineteen-forties and at some point they found a crate. "This crate even had barnacles all over it," in Miel's words. The fishermen hoisted the crate out of the water and they noticed there were some letters printed on top, R.A.F., the initials of the British air force. Opening the box, they got a surprise. It was full of cookies and chocolate.

"We couldn't believe it," you hear Miel say, "what with the shape we were in and how hungry we'd been, we polished off those cookies in nothing flat."

But the amusement didn't stop there. After eating the cookies, the fishermen couldn't get to sleep. They went the whole day without any sleep, on the second day as well they didn't shut their eyes. And what's more, they were all set for work, as if they'd slept a full eight hours. On the third day, though, they couldn't keep their eyes open. A three days' drowsiness suddenly overcame them. "I slept twenty-four hours straight." It seems the chocolate and cookies had been meant for the fighter pilots, and contained some kind of drug so they could stay awake through the long hours of their missions.

The part about the R.A.F. crate reminded me of something our mother used to tell. Back in those times, Basque fishermen would often find flotsam from shipwrecks in the sea. Rubber was the most prized of all. Ashore, rubber brought in much more money than fish did. They used to find bales of rubber floating in the water. They'd slice up these bales with sisal twine and hide the pieces in their duffel bags to sell on the black market.

Before the Second World War, rubber was extracted from trees, first in Brazil, then in Malaysia and Indochina. The Brazilians had kept guard over their rubber trees as if they were gold but British and French spies stole seeds and began cultivating them in their Asian colonies. In 1942 the campaign in the Pacific left the U.S. forces without any raw materials for making rubber, and that's when the real race to obtain synthetic rubber began.

For freighters attempting to cross the Atlantic 1942 and 1943 were difficult years. These ships were easy for the German submarines to send to the bottom. Between 1941 and 1944 the coast from Hendaye all the way up to North Cape was under German control.

Granddad found bales of rubber once when he was fishing the French coast. Vestiges of a wreck. Our mother vividly remembers the day he appeared with the new shoes he'd bought with the money from that rubber. He brought home a pair for each of the daughters.

Miel also tells what happened to them once over Galicia way. They were on the lookout for bonito tuna there. Since the coasting was going quite long it occurred to the captain to paint the boat. They put the vessel into dry dock and started painting, the fishermen themselves. That sparked a great deal of curiosity. Every day a small crowd came down to see the boat. The fishermen didn't understand why, since when it came down to it theirs was just an inshore boat much like the ones they had in Galicia. A bit later the matter got clarified. It was a widespread belief in the area that Basque boats had glass bottoms and that's why the Basques caught fish to the extent they did. The people were coming to get a look at that glass bottom.

The boats out of Basque ports were in all likelihood no faster than any others and their overall catch, too, was probably about even. But distance always tends to beget mystery, myth.

The atmosphere of those years when Miel first came to town also turns up on the tape. There was no lighting in the town, in the early hours of the morning the municipal night watchmen went from house to house to rouse people, and a bit afterward you'd hear nothing but the sound of sabots in the streets. They all wore those wooden shoes. Once at sea, on the other hand, they'd go barefoot. On feast days they wore espadrilles.

The way fishing has changed is collected here as well. In those early years the catch was divvied up among the boats, Miel says. Likewise, when it was anchovy season the fish was handed out to the whole town. "They'd toss a kerchief up from the wharf to one of us crew and we'd hand down a kerchief of anchovies to whoever'd come asking for them. There was immense solidarity at that time. Nowadays, that solidarity is gone."

The day she lent me the recording, as we were saying goodbye his widow began to weep, "He's left a huge empty place in me, he was such a good man. I hardly leave the house since he died." By what Miel's wife said, he'd been sad and at loose ends when he took his retirement and left the sea. He didn't know what to do, he missed that life at sea. At some point, he suddenly took up an old avocation, painting. He spent hours and hours painting, at the kitchen table. He'd put a knee on a chair and paint like that. With the same talent his father had had for engraving paper money.

"He was a very cheerful man," Antigua said to me when she'd dried her tears. He was stricken with an aneurism and they operated on him. Not long after that the whole clan had a family dinner. Just to be on the safe side, Miel stayed behind at home, he was feeling weak and it was just better to stay home.

Miel couldn't stand not going to the dinner, though. He put on a clown mask and set off for the house where the family was dining. Just next door to his own. He wanted to give them a surprise. But as he began climbing the stairs he felt unwell.

One of the children found him on the stairs. "That's how we lost him, just as he always was, with that sense of humor of his."

I look at the navigator on the screen. A map of the Atlantic has appeared there. Europe and America in their entirety. And a parabola charts the plane's trajectory from when it left Frankfurt to where it's crossed the British Isles. We still haven't made it even half of the way. The screen also displays precisely where the day is. The countries where it's night show up darkened and those where it's daylight are light. When we left Frankfurt Europe was light and the western coast of the United States in darkness. Now shadow is spreading over Europe and light in the Pacific.

Time does that kind of work. Inside us, too, parts that were darkened suddenly get lit up. Parts that were dark when you were young light up as you mature. When you're young a few things are hugely important, friends are important, nighttime is important, ideals are important. And a few other, different kinds of matters you leave totally out of the picture. Even what they are. Fatherhood, to name an example. That continent was totally in darkness for me until now. But now it's getting lighter, daytime is spreading out over a previously unseen glorious country. And, in the same way, nighttime is coming to several other places, as if by fate.

14

NUUK

Distance to Destination: 2,061 miles
Time to destination: 4:04 hours
Local Time: 03:15 PM
Ground Speed: 506 mph
Altitude: 35,000
Outside air temperature: -67°, F
Reykjavik, Godthåb, St. John's

The young guys in the jazz shirts ask L. Thompson the flight attendant for a third round of vodkas, laughing uproariously. L. Thompson tells them no. They try again as flight attendant S. Usko is passing by. S. Usko says no as well. That we had supper ages ago.

"They look so happy. At our place there's already none of that joyousness," Renata says to me, taking off her headphones. "The kids left to go off to college. Both have their own lives. Do you have any children yourself?"

"Yes, my wife's son lives at home with us."

"How old is he?"

"Sixteen."

"Not a baby anymore, then."

"Nerea had Unai when she was very young. When she went to Denmark to study."

"How did you meet each other?"

"We're from the same town. But we never got together until three years ago."

"Yeah, our lives take us off on different tracks a lot of times. When we least expect it something happens in your life, somebody suddenly shows up, and your life is utterly transformed."

"But fears show up, too, at those same moments. It scared me to fall in love with Nerea. I knew it was going to happen but it made me dizzy."

No sooner did I finish the sentence than I suddenly remembered the painter Aurelio Arteta. I don't know if Arteta, too, felt dizzy when they asked him to paint the picture of the bombing of Guernica for the pavilion the Spanish Republic was going to have at the International Exposition in Paris. It's anyone's guess. The only thing I know is that in the end he decided to go to Mexico with his family, leaving the war behind. And that's what's most important right now.

Arteta underwent terrible hardships during the war. His eldest son was conscripted by the National troops. Yet he himself was active in the resistance. Alongside numerous other intellectuals he set in motion the "Manifesto Against the War" in Barcelona, joining with Antonio Machado, Luis Cernuda, Miguel Hernández, Maria Zambrano.

By that time all of his pictures had to do with the war. The war over and over again.

Sick of the infighting among the Republic's supporters, in 1938 he finally determined to go to Mexico, with his wife and two small sons. There Francisco Belausteguigoitia and Elvira Arocena took him in. They had an entire hotel to give asylum to the exiles who were leaving the Basque Country.

Arteta had married a second time, to Amalia Barredo, in 1929. Amalia had been the painter's model and friend for many long years and they went and got married at last. Amalia had one son from before, Andres, and together they had another, Aurelio.

On November 10, 1940, Arteta learned that one of his closest friends had been shot. He thought the best thing for him to do would be to go up to the mountains, to deal with the worst of his grief far from the city clamor. With that intention, the couple caught a streetcar. They were in an accident. Arteta, near death, had time to write a short note saying goodbye to his family. Then he died. He'd wanted to escape death, and death, where he least expected it, caught up with him. "Wherever you go, there you'll die," our mother says.

One of the first to go view the body was Indalecio Prieto, who was also in Mexico in those years. Prieto truly admired Arteta. There are no letters between the two of them.

The Artetas had been afraid and burned them all.

Seeking to respond to the Francoist air corps's bombing of the city and unable to contain their fury, the inhabitants of Republican Bilbao staged an assault on the city's jails on January 4, 1937, at five in the afternoon. They intended to kill the National Front prisoners who were held in them. One of those jails was the Larrinaga jail.

The authorities made some kind of an attempt to stem the attack but it was too late. Hundreds of people died that afternoon. One of the prisoners serving time in the Larrinaga jail was our grandfather Liborio. He piled the bodies of the dead on top of himself and hid. That's how he escaped death. Then, taking advantage of the chaos, he fled up through Begoña into the mountains.

As he was going up Begoña, however, a skinny little fellow named Jose Luis Meler who was escaping along with him was hit by sharpshooters.

Liborio took him up in a fireman's carry and hauled him to a safe place.

—

To find out how they took the *Toki-Argia* under guard, Dad's friend Jon Akarregi told me, the best thing for me to do would be to talk with Isidor Etxebarria. Akarregi had been fishing for bonito on the factory trawlers off Angola. He'd spent a lot of time on the fishing grounds there. But he'd also made trips out to Rockall with Dad.

On one of those trips Dad told him the story of how they'd hauled them off to Stornoway the first time. These were their initial trips up around Rockall, back in the far-off nineteen-seventies, and Justo Larrinaga and our dad had gone to test out the tackle. One time a coast-guard cutter moved in on them. That was the inaugural occasion. The inflatable tender came up to the side and the cutter's captain ordered them to lower their ladder. Justo said no, not to lower it. The captain, for a second time: Send it down. He was checking them out through his binoculars. Justo said no. The third time, they said "Off to Stornoway," and escorted them to the port.

That was the very first time they set foot in Stornoway. On that occasion nothing happened. They were set free without delay. But the occasion that turns up in Miel's picture was much different. They had a trial and everything. At home I'd heard something, but I wanted the details.

The attorney Isidor Etxebarria handled the cases of those vessels that had been taken in charge.

As soon as we entered his house in San Sebastian the lawyer showed Nerea and me a newspaper. "Look what's in the paper," he said to us, gesturing at the obituary page.

SEVENTH-DAY MASS AND IN THANKSGIVING

Fabian Larrauri Astuy

"ASMOR"

(R.I.P.)

Departed this life on June 17, 2008, at age 87, in
the blessing of the Church and the Holy Father

HIS FAMILY MEMBERS

Express their warmest gratitude to all who
sent their condolences and attended the holy
rites of the Church on behalf of his soul

Fabian Larrauri was the owner of the *Toki-Argia*. "Here the very day you come to talk with me about the *Toki-Argia* his death notice appears. It's been years since I've heard anything at all and look, I get two pieces of news on the same day."

Isidor Etxebarria had gotten everything he had to tell us superlatively well prepared. Before laying out how they'd captured the vessel he told us what the general jurisdiction had been like in those days. "There were in those days over a hundred draggers in Ondarroa port." And then, he began to tell us about fishing rights. "At the outset of things, territorial waters extended no more than three miles out. Beyond three miles, the ocean belonged to everyone."

The way they marked out the territorial waters was weird. The specification went according to the firing power of a cannon set up on shore. However far a cannonball could reach would be marked as territorial waters. Little by little, cannons went on improving and what at first had been three miles was later six, and still a bit later nine.

In 1976 they set it at two hundred miles. At the time, the countries that made up the European Union set the figure, Great Britain among them. The fishing code made its way to Brussels. Waters that down through the years had been free to all became European, and so did the waters around Rockall island where our dad used to work.

For the two-hundred-mile law to be in effect on an island it was necessary for people to live on it. Nobody has ever lived on Rockall, since that's impossible. People did live on St. Kilda, however. Up until the nineteen-thirties people had lived there. And since Rockall lies within two hundred miles of the islands of St. Kilda, you now couldn't fish there without a permit.

In the spring of 1982 a British naval plane took a photograph of the *Toki-Argia* as they fished without a permit off Rockall, and sent notification of the fact to the court in Brussels and to the coast guard in Stornoway. Since the *Toki-Argia* was by then already on its way home, they'd have to bide their time until the next trip to go out in search of the vessel.

Days went by and again the *Toki-Argia* was plying the waters off Rockall, fishing. Around about then, the captain of the cutter *Jura*, Ratery was his name, caught up with the *Toki-Argia* and took her in to Stornoway port under guard.

The fine was forty thousand pounds and once it was paid they let the fishermen go, to await trial. What people had done up until then was admit they were guilty, pay the fine and head back home. The boats' names would get sent to Brussels and there put onto a blacklist. As a result, they would lose their permission to make the next scheduled trip out.

Isidor had luck on his side in the case of the *Toki-Argia*. The trial was delayed unexpectedly, the two British pilots had gone off to the Malvinas and couldn't take part in the trial until they were back from the war. That stretch of time gave the lawyer a chance to think, and to better his defence. The usual thing was for them to confess they were guilty and pay the fine, but this time he was going to be preparing a true defence.

The defence was going to hinge on this: the vessel in the aerial photograph wasn't the *Toki-Argia*, it was another boat. In actual fact, Brussels kept vessels that had been caught fishing illegally on its blacklist and didn't give them permission to put to sea. But all of the *Toki-Argia*'s paperwork was in order on May 22, 1982, when the *Jura* caught up with her. For one thing, she had the fishing permit right on board, and what's more, was not on the Brussels blacklist. As a matter of fact, it had slipped Brussels' mind to put a sea ban on the *Toki-Argia*. Etxebarria took advantage of that bureaucratic slipup.

Etxebarria told our dad to plead not guilty before the Stornoway sheriff. Scott, the procurator fiscal, however, insisted they were guilty, and to prove it he also brought in the two R.A.F. pilots to testify.

"Not guilty" was the verdict at the last. It was the first trial Etxebarria had ever won. Everyone who'd taken part in the trial was on the flight from Stornoway to Glasgow together. It was such a small aircraft they all ended up in conversation. One of the pilots from the Malvinas told our dad, in English, smiling, *You know you were there.* Dad smiled right back at him.

The trial presents still another weird aspect. Since they'd already paid the forty-thousand-pound fine, the Scottish authorities had to send the money back to Larrauri Bros.

The thing is, the currency in those days, the peseta, had gone down in the meantime and the Larrauris of Bermeo ended up making some money out of the deal.

"If you're going to Stornoway ask after Angus MacLeod," Etxebarria said before bidding us goodbye at the door. "He's the one who will tell you more about this."

15

ST. KILDA

The islands of St. Kilda are the landmass closest to Rockall. Up until 1930 people did live there. The very last inhabitants left just then, a two-thousand-year-old way of life ended just then, on the 28th of August in 1930 to be exact, when one sunny day they packed up their things and left the islands forever. There were fewer than forty in the town at the time, the young people had already left in search of new terrains and only the older folks remained on the islands.

The traces of human life on St. Kilda, though, date from long, long before, from the Neolithic. For the last five hundred years the islands belonged to the MacLeod family. Once a year the landowner's representative would make the trip to the main island, in summer. He'd collect the rent then and bring the islanders the things they needed. It's odd to see what things the island's inhabitants asked for. They asked for cows and tools, but also for clothing. On one of these lists you could see how they'd asked for a dozen men's-size berets.

Their relationship with fashion on that remote island is striking. At the end of the nineteenth century wealthy tourists arrived there in the summers. It was exotic to travel to the farthest-off island in Great Britain. Once, a woman was stunned speechless as she came ashore in St. Kilda port and saw an island woman wearing the very latest clothes from London's Oxford Street. That island woman was dressed more up-to-the-minute than the tourists who'd arrived on the ship. When asked how she'd come by these clothes the woman reportedly responded that she'd swapped for them with a tourist the summer before. The island woman wanted to be more up-to-the-minute than anyone.

Through the centuries that yearly boat had been the sole link the island's inhabitants had with the civilised world. To send mail they used to build small wooden boats, as if they were play ones, toys. Inside they'd put the letter and a penny and throw it into the sea with a few explanatory notes. The boat would have "PLEASE OPEN" written on the outside.

They'd put the little boat in the water on a day when there was a northwest wind, and it would come ashore in northern Scotland or Norway. They began using the little mail boats in 1877.

In February of that year the Austrian barque *Peti Dubrovacki* was shipwrecked and the St. Kildans saved all the sailors. But as the winter progressed their food went on dwindling and the mail-boat idea occurred to one John Sands. The mail boat was addressed to the consul that Austria had in Glasgow. Nine days later they received it in Scotland and took the letter to the consul.

The vessel HMS *Jackal* appeared off St. Kilda a few days afterward and took the stranded Austrian sailors aboard.

The twentieth century brought change to St. Kilda. Their two-thousand-year-old way of life ended right then. Through the centuries the islanders had lived from animal husbandry and the feathers of birds. But the coming of tourism changed that way of life down to the ground. They gave up tilling the soil, plucking the seabirds and sheep-herding and they set their sights on tourism. They forgot the way of life of earlier times.

Until they left the island, that is.

The decision to quit the island was bought about by an illness. And yet it wasn't a grave illness. A mere case of appendicitis impelled their leaving the island. In January of 1930 a woman named Mary Gillies came down with a stomachache. A freighter was in port just then and notice was sent that a lady was ill. They didn't get her to Glasgow hospital until February 15th. That's where the woman died.

The inhabitants took Mary's death very hard and, gathered in assembly according to the customs of old, decided to leave the island. By then, no more than fifteen men and twenty-two women lived there. Because the rest had decided to emigrate, to America or to Australia.

The oldest inhabitants didn't want to abandon the island, they told their families to leave them there, right there is where they wanted to die, they said, alongside their dead friends and relations.

From what people tell, the St. Kildans adapted very poorly to their new way of life. They never forgot the life they'd had on that remote and stormy island.

I look at the screen to see what there is to see there. I turn first to the music section. I click on "Norah Jones Live." Norah Jones appears, playing piano in a theatre. Percussion and bass. The Brooklyn-born singer begins to sing.

> *I waited 'til I saw the sun.*
> *I don't know why I didn't come.*
> *I left you by the house of fun.*
> *I don't know why I didn't come.*
> *I don't know why I didn't come.*

I look around at the people on the plane. Most all of them are sleeping. Renata too. There are people from a lot of the world's countries in this cabin together. In May I went to lunch in New York with Fiona, who had published my book of poems. We'd arranged to meet at an Italian restaurant called Fiorello's. It's directly across from Lincoln Center, on Broadway. There are little plaques on the tables with people's full names on them. Such a one used to sit at this table, this table is another family's private spot. The restaurant was full to overflowing. People who'd just come out of the opera.

I laid out the project of the novel to Fiona. The idea had gone on evolving, I said, and finally I'd be setting everything on a flight between Bilbao and New York. How else would I talk about three generations of a family without going back to some nineteenth-century novel. I told her about the process of writing the novel and in bits, in very small bits, stories of the three generations.

"That's just the way I live, too, on an airplane," Fiona said to me, first thing. "I'm from Scotland, my office is in St. Paul and my husband's from New York."

Some people live on airplanes, others on boats. Just recently they found a sailor drowned in the harbor, at home in Ondarroa. The event took place near-obliviously. The sailor was an immigrant and was living right on the boat. His full name was even on file but he had no house. The boat he worked on was his residence. When someone needed to find him they had to go to the launch. Nobody knows for sure how the man drowned, it looks as if he was trying to get aboard and slipped. A matter of bad luck. And he lost his life between the iron-hulled vessels. Nothing's really clear, though. That man was living right on the boat but he's not the only one, strange as it might seem. Even today a lot of seamen live on their boats. They work there, and make their lives there, too, even when their vessel's in port. They come ashore from time to time, make a trip to the taverns, leave their solitude behind them for a while, and at night go on back to the boat to sleep.

The way of life of those seamen who have no homes strikes me as horrible. They live aboard and put down no roots at all ashore. The boat's in the harbor, on the water, afloat, and the sailor tends not to cross the border, as if he had no desire to bind his life to that port town. His residence is provisional. His house isn't built on land. The supporting beams of his house are not firm. Neither here nor there, always on the water.

Some, a few, do cross that wharfside border, though. Once, when I was in Andalucia on vacation, something weird happened to me. I started talking with a couple of young people and when I said where I was from, one of them told me that he, too, had lived in Ondarroa when he was little. Life's coincidences. His parents, when they first reached the Basque Country, had had no home and used to sleep in the port-side warehouses. They made their bed there among the nets. That's what he told me. And that his oldest sister had been born right there, in the warehouse among the nets, as if she were a little mermaid, fishery smell and all. After spending a few years working on the Basque coast they all then returned to Andalucia. Or not all of them, the sister stayed in the Basque Country.

There are people who have managed to leave the boat and the port and take a house. At the outset they settled in to live with a few other sailors, then on their own. After a couple of years. A few among those ones even got married, and had children. Those children speak Basque nowadays.

When the subject of immigration comes up I often remember the harbor seamen. And I think the image of the harbor could clarify our discussion about immigrants' integration. Some stay on the boat, in that non-place. Others cross over to the port town and, finally, there are some who put down roots in the new ground.

The image could be useful, it's true, but I suspect the business of integration is most times not a matter of will. Since, most times, the entry to the harbor is closed. I leave the music section and go into film on the plane screen. I've got a choice of four movies:

Entre les murs. France. 128 min. Laurent Cantet (François Bégaudeau, Nassim Amrabt, Laura Baquela). *Delta.* Hungary. 92 min. Kornél Mundruczó (Félix Lajkó, Orsolya Tóth, Lili Monori). *Changeling.* USA. 140 min. Clint Eastwood (Angelina Jolie, John Malkovich, Jeffrey Donovan). *The Tale of*

Desperaux. USA/UK. 90 min. Sam Fell, Robert Stevenhagen, Gary Ross.

I choose the first film, *Entre les murs.*

ENTRE LES MURS (THE CLASS) France. 128 min.

Laurent Cantet (François Bégaudeau, Nassim Amrabt, Laura Baquela)

2008. Cannes Festival: Palme D'Or / Drama / SYNOPSIS: François is a teacher of French in a public secondary school in a conflict-ridden neighbourhood. His students are between the ages of 14 and 15. François will argue with Esmeralda, Souleymane, Khoumba and the rest of his students over what language is and isn't.

The movie's a fiction film that looks like a documentary. Twenty-four young people are its protagonists. Not one is a professional actor. The teenagers are studying their mandatory second language at the Collège D'enseignement Général Françoise Dolto in Paris.

A click on the screen and the film begins. You hear a siren and in the classroom a teacher slamming a hand on a desk to silence the students. On the screen the logo of the Cannes Palme D'Or. Students asking the teacher questions. *Entre les murs* (The Class). Students in a rage at one another. *Un film de Laurent Cantet.* Students in the schoolyard. *Librement adapté du roman de François Bégaudeau.* Teachers arguing in the teachers' lounge. *Entre les murs.*

The students are Unai's age. I can recall the day he sent me a text message for the first time. Immense joy. Over the months I had been sending him messages. Commonplace messages, informational data. I'll be there at such-and-such a time, at such another time we'll go over your homework. He'd receive them, sure, but not a single answer. Until one day he finally answered me. The content of the message is immaterial, something like "Ok" or "Will b there." But getting the message itself was truly important to me.

Our dad got sick on September 2nd. That was the last time our folks went to the movies. We took a photo of them before they left the house. The last photo of the two of them together. On the way home he felt unwell. They took him to the hospital. Pancreatitis. A few days hospitalised, then into the intensive care unit. We'd go to visit him every day. Half hour in the mornings, half hour in the afternoons. Normally he'd talk to us, even if he was feeling down.

On one of these visits Dad told us he'd gone over his life and there was one thing he was happy about and one thing he regretted. He was happy because in all those long years that he'd spent at sea he hadn't lost a single man. No one had ever died on him, he'd got all of them back home trip after trip, even though they'd run in some extreme waves.

The only thing he regretted, he'd once hauled off and throttled his father.

16

A MESSAGE ON FACEBOOK

That man who when he had a scant few months to live took our mum to the museum, that man who used to gather the kids around him and tell them stories, the allegedly good and openhanded man, was in Larrinaga jail, apparently, for having come down on the side of the fascist uprising. At first I found that hard to take. I couldn't comprehend it.

But then I saw that in a person's life the surrounding terrain takes on great weight and that those surroundings condition the decisions that get made. And that these decisions can even be wrong.

When I first took up the idea of the novel, I found the Granddad Liborio character simultaneously attractive and uncomfortable. My own grandfather had himself come down on the side of the fascist uprising, on the side of the movement that brought those bloodbaths into being. I could have talked, no doubt of it at all, about my other grandfather, Mum's father. Hipolito Urbieta, a calm and canny man, who together with so many other men had had to flee, on the eve of the day the National Front soldiers took the town, near dawn. He had to flee leaving his wife and daughters all by themselves. Grandma Anparo, that intrepid woman who faced off against the Italian soldiers wielding an axe.

I could talk about Hipolito and suppress Liborio's story. Still and all, for the novel Liborio was far more attractive to me. A person full of contradictions, who raised so many questions for me. Why did that man who spoke barely any Spanish take the side of the uprising? Why did he take Franco's side knowing that his own brother, Domingo, had come down on the Republican side? What was the true reason that impelled him to make that decision?

I will never know.

Still and all, or precisely because of that, I felt the need to tell Liborio's story, I wanted to speak that reality that had been silenced so many times. The civil war was also a war between Basques. It wasn't solely an invasion of Francoist troops. What happened is more complicated than that. And I had to say that, had to verbalise it, to say with no possibility of mistaking that our grandfather had taken Franco's side, Liborio Uribe, even if in my opinion his choice was wrong.

While Granddad Liborio was in jail Grandmother Ana had a year-old baby, our dad, and she was pregnant with our uncle. She was alone at home and scarcely able to go to the jail to visit her husband. That responsibility fell to Aunt Maritxu. She took him his food and clean clothing, without fail.

Aunt Maritxu told me that they put Granddad in jail because of envy, animosities in town. She said evil had outweighed politics. He turned up on a list of monarchists and someone turned him in.

Santi Meabe the bird-trainer gave the order to jail our grandfather.

What's more, Aunt said, once he was released from jail he didn't want to know anything about anything. That same Jose Luis Meler, the man he'd saved from Larrinaga jail, promised Liborio he'd help him obtain a good position in society, and would get money for him, too, if he wanted. But Liborio never asked him for any money at all.

In the house at 12 North Street, Commandant Velarde Street back then, each room was painted a different colour, the way they do in the La Boca barrio of Buenos Aires, using paint left over from the boats.

In addition to our grandparents and their children there were two other people they'd given houseroom there. Both of them spent their days at the jail at Saturraran. One was the military man Javier and the other was Carmen, from Asturias, the daughter of a prisoner. As if those two weren't enough, they were also giving food to Carmen's mother. Twelve North Street was the address Carmen had on her slip of paper when she reached Ondarroa for the first time.

Carmen was deeply startled when she got off the bus and saw all the men walking around dressed in blue coveralls. She had a terrible fright. She thought the whole town was Falangist, instead of realizing they were fishermen.

"Go to this address and ask after Joxpantoni." Joxpantoni Osa was Liborio's mother. She was a big woman, powerful, and had made a third marriage with our great-grandfather Jose Uribe. Even now at home we have a photograph of her. Great-grandmother Joxpantoni is down at the port, mending anchovy nets, along with several other women. Compared with the other ladies Joxpantoni is robust, she looks like a giant, almost.

The one was tall and powerful and the other was teeny-tiny. Great-grandfather Jose was short and skinny. "I may be small, all right, but at long last I managed to get Big Joxpantoni to marry me," he used to say proudly. Even though theirs was a third marriage for her, he was as proud as could be.

I don't know the exact circumstances but Communist Party people had told Carmen to go to that North Street house. I don't know who her contact would have been, who would have sent her there.

But to speak the truth, where else would she be safer than in a war hero's house?

—

I like a small museum in New York. It's not as well-known as MOMA or the Metropolitan but it's really worth going to. It's a museum constructed on a human scale. Because, in essence, it's a house. It sits to one side of Central Park. In it is the art collection of the industrialist Henry Clay Frick.

Pictures by well-known artists are all over the place there, Goya, Vermeer, Turner, Monet and others. The museum was a residence and the pictures are scattered throughout the various rooms. In the living room is the picture by Giovanni Bellini titled "St. Francis in the Desert." Painted in 1480, it shows the day St. Francis saw the light. That saint who knew the language of the birds. Father St. Francis is gazing up at the sky, and beside him are a donkey and a flock of sheep, who are meanwhile conscious of none of it.

But the weirdest thing about this artwork is a bit of paper painted into one corner. The wind has carried the paper to the left side of the saint's hut. On the paper it says "Giovanni Bellini." The artist's own name appears in the picture.

That detail gave me something to think about. How I had to deal with the narration of the novel. How to speak about those closest to me without appearing myself. I had to talk about my grandfather, my father, my mother. Put my world on the page. But how to do that? Was I supposed to invent a set of mendacious names or was I myself going to appear in the novel as storyteller?

Bellini's picture isn't the only painting in which a maker's name appears. A few years earlier, in 1434, the painter Jan Van Eyck inserted a sentence into one of his best-known pictures. Namely, in "The Arnolfini Marriage." And so this is what Van Eyck wrote in his painting: "Johannes de Eyck fuit hic 1434." Van Eyck was here in 1434. In its day the Flemish painter's work was a total revolution. It was the first time that a scene from a bourgeois couple's daily life had been painted. The husband and wife are in their bedroom, some house slippers are scattered around, and there's a little dog too. On the back wall of the bedroom is a mirror, a convex mirror, and in the mirror the husband and wife appear seen from behind.

Inspired by Van Eyck's mirror, Diego Velázquez composed his well-known picture *Las Meninas,* in 1656. Velázquez, too, made use of the mirror game but in another way. Velázquez's leap forward was that the scene in the picture itself didn't appear in the mirror, the way it did in Van Eyck's. Velázquez turns the picture around. And the scene he's allegedly painting appears in the mirror, that is, the portrait of the king and queen. In fact, in the *Meninas* picture Velázquez is painting a portrait of the royal couple, and their daughter and all the rest are watching them. Somehow, Velázquez shows us the picture's insides, what's on the picture's other side –

painting those who stand watching, instead of the king and queen.

In *Las Meninas* the other side of a picture appears. The author himself appears, Velázquez, painting a picture. What's happening while the picture is being painted appears. The king and queen stand posing and a number of people are looking on. And in the background is the hazy image of that picture he will paint, the king and queen in the mirror. *Las Meninas* makes visible a picture's insides and I reasoned that I had to tell the story of what's inside a novel. The interviews that get done, the work in the archives, the research work on the Internet. To put on display: all the doubts entertained and the wrong roads taken. On display: how the author himself has changed since beginning to write the novel.

And just as in Velázquez's work the image of the picture being painted appears hazy, in the novel, too, the reader will only suspect what kind of novel the author is writing. The novel itself will never appear per se. Nevertheless, one must not forget that what's most important in *Las Meninas* are the *meninas,* the young ladies-in-waiting, and not the royal couple. And not Velázquez himself. And in my novel, too, what's most important will not be that still-unwritten novel, what's most important isn't the writer, but the flight itself. I mean, the movement is the most important thing, the process that leads the writer to write the novel.

I didn't want to construct any fictional characters, I wanted to talk about real people.

In the summer of this year I read in the press an interview they'd done with Meryl Streep. She'd come for the San Sebastian Film Festival and the press people had a question for her. "What's the best question we could ask you and what is its answer?" Streep answered without thinking twice. "Is fiction of any use nowadays?" That was the question she cared about. And her answer was: "If it tells about real things, yes."

On September 12th of this year, the writer David Foster Wallace killed himself. His wife found him the next day. He was only forty-seven. The book *Infinite Jest* made Wallace famous worldwide, a book of over a thousand pages. In the novel Wallace is writing about the future, how years, instead of being given numbers as has been done up to now, 2008 for instance, will in the future be given the names of sponsors, "Depends, the year of the adult undergarment."

Wallace was an innovator, he loved to experiment, but in one of his last interviews he said this: "Emotion is fundamental. What's written has got to be alive, and, though I don't know all that well how to explain it, it's a very tender thing. Starting in ancient Greece, good writing puts a knot in your stomach. Everything else is worthless for anything."

I had a message on Facebook from the writer Kevin MacNeil. "It's too bad, I'm going to be out of town for those days, in the Shetland Islands." MacNeil was the writer from Stornoway. Jamieson had given me a book of his in Estonia, a book of short texts and poems. To fall in with an old plan of our mother's, we decided in June to go to Stornoway and I wrote to Alan Jamieson in Edinburgh. I asked him who we could talk to in Stornoway. We wanted someone to show us the town, to get to know the area from closer to.

Alan's reply was instantaneous and direct: Talk to Kevin MacNeil.

MacNeil connects storytelling to burglary. Writing is as stimulating and risky as stealing. In the book Alan gave me Kevin tells that his father was a thief. He had extremely quick fingers, so quick he ate even his soup with his fingers.

When young Kevin realised his dad was getting old, he wanted to learn his craft. He asked his father to show him the art of stealing. His dad was overjoyed. He took his son to this one house.

They leapt over the iron fence, got into the house, and found a large trunk there. His father said to him, "Get in there and don't go moaning about the risk. Just take the most elegant piece of clothing." When he'd got inside his dad closed the trunk, and went off, jumping out a window. Then he beat on the front door. Everyone in the house woke up. Kevin's father leapt over the iron fence and fled.

There Kevin was, in the trunk, unable to make a sound and cursing his dad. But then the light dawned. He began making the kind of sound that mice make in the garret. Hearing it, the father of the house told his son to look and see if any mice were scrabbling around inside that trunk. As soon as the householder's son opened the trunk Kevin blew out the flame of the candle he held. And that was the way Kevin got out of the trunk, in the pitch dark.

But he knew that everyone in the house would soon be hunting for him. He glanced out the window and saw a puddle just below it. He tossed a stone into the puddle. The people of the house thought the burglar was escaping.

Once he'd in fact escaped and got back home Kevin found his dad waiting up for him. He was sitting there with a glass in his hand and beaming from ear to ear. "You've learned the art!" he said, and gave another glass to Kevin to toast with. That's when Kevin decided he'd be not a thief but a writer.

The Facebook message went on like this: "If as you say you want to talk with one of those old fishermen, go down to the pubs in the port. But watch it, go to the ones that say 'Bar' and not the ones that say 'Lounge.' The real fishermen never, ever go to the lounges. Good luck!"

We paid attention to Kevin and went into a pub when we were in Stornoway, one of those that said 'Bar.' I don't remember the name of the place. It had no name of any kind on the outside. There was a small card next to the red-painted door: "This pub is not just for drinking. People who come to read the papers are also welcome." But inside no one was reading. Drinking, though, yes.

Alan Jamieson had commanded me to buy three books. One of Kevin's: *The Stornoway Way*. We tried in Stornoway and found nothing. Instead, I bought a Scottish classic, *Tales and Travels of a School Inspector*. Which tells of the visits the schoolmaster John Wilson made to Scottish village schools in the nineteenth century.

Wilson spent time in Stornoway. He tells a lot of things about the nineteenth-century way of life there. To Wilson's eye, Stornoway was a large town, the largest on the island, but the teachers who went there had great difficulty in understanding the students of the place and vice versa. The children spoke Gaelic and the teachers knew only English.

During the days Wilson spent in Stornoway a strange occurrence took place. Half an hour from Stornoway, on the northern tip of the Isle of Lewis, is a lighthouse. The fishermen were startled, because one morning they'd noticed the lighthouse was also lit by day. They were afraid something might have happened to the lightman. They went into the lighthouse and found the lightman dead. A burglary, to all appearances. The lighthouse itself had betrayed what had happened to the lightman. The way a dog does howling when its master takes sick.

In Wilson's book I found one thing quite striking: the Scots believed that Gaelic had been Tubal's language, just the way we Basques had done.

17

IN THE MIDDLE OF THE ATLANTIC

A boat's captain gets hardly any sleep. He tends to be up long hours. That's precisely how it happened that night to a friend's father too. He was running in a factory vessel out of Bermeo, two hundred miles or so off the African coast. At night, he put in the coordinates, set the autopilot and went to his berth to have a three- or four-hour nap.

A catnap, one eye shut and one eye open, in case anything happened.

The vessel would be making headway at low throttle. While he was sleeping, something unexpected woke him. The boat stopped. He couldn't believe it, since they were in the middle of the ocean.

The autopilot might conceivably have broken down, and the waves would take the vessel coastward. The dead stop, though, hadn't been jarring at all. The vessel hadn't let out any great noise when she stopped. And if they'd struck a submerged rock she would have let out some kind of noise. He looked from the bridge and nothing was visible in the dark night, not a rock, and not a glimpse of shore. Sky above, water below.

He went to the bow of the vessel and noticed something dark on the surface. He backed water and discovered the reason the vessel had stopped.

It was a whale, chopped right in two.

The fisherman couldn't believe it. What was that whale doing there anyhow, why hadn't it got out of the boat's way, as they usually did? Then and there he understood that the whale had killed itself, and where but in the middle of the ocean.

This aircraft is crossing the Atlantic like a whale. A little girl runs past beside me. She knocks into my shoulder. Comes back and apologises. She's blond and wears glasses. *Little Miss Sunshine.* She reminds me of the movie's protagonist. We saw that movie in San Sebastian at the Principe multiplex. Nerea, Unai and myself. Unai didn't want to see that movie. He thought it was for little kids. His mother told him yes, he was going to go. Cross as sticks, but we went in at last. When we went in we found the movie theatre empty. We had to sit waiting for a very, very long half hour. Just what we needed. What with the argument at the theatre door we'd misread the time. The wait turned out shorter than we'd thought it would. We ate corn chips.

Unai liked the movie no end.

I had to be at Bar Six at seven to meet Elizabeth in May of this year. I caught the A train at Fifty-ninth Street and needed to get off three stops farther downtown, at the Fourteenth Street stop. From the subway stop Bar Six is barely a stone's throw away. Not being sure how to judge the distances I got there a quarter hour early. I ordered a beer at the bar. I looked through the newspapers and magazines on the rack by the bar and picked out that week's issue of *The New Yorker*. To look at the cartoons.

"¿Cómo usted por acá?" the barman asked me in Spanish. What brings you here? He was Colombian, was studying acting, he said. From my looks he'd apparently sensed I knew Spanish. We chatted about his country, about Colombian writing.

On the stroke of seven Elizabeth came into the bar. Seeing me in conversation with the barman, she said, "How quickly you've gotten to be a New Yorker."

We were going to supper at the home of Jose Fernandez de Albornoz and Scott Hightower. In New York's Chelsea. The apartment was spectacular, a duplex. On the lower story the living room, kitchen and bedroom. Climb some little stairs and up there was the library, and a door leading from the library onto a terrace.

From the terrace you could see the New York night, the lights of the buildings. "The moon's broodlings." In *Poet in New York* Lorca called them exactly that.

The house was scattered with pictures and antique

furniture. Among the pictures were a drawing of Jean Cocteau's and an etching of Picasso's. "People used to be able to pick up Picasso etchings for next to nothing at flea markets, back in the day," Jose said to me.

The picture I loved most, in any case, they had hanging in the living room. It was full of reds and oranges. Best of all, though, was the picture's history. Scott, when he was young, had fled his native Texas, carrying only a backpack and a picture. In the backpack his clothing and food. The picture was a friend's, to sell in case he got into some tight corner.

He never sold it.

As I looked at that untitled picture I thought it was the very picture that best laid out my own experiences to date. If Granddad's picture was Arteta's mural, and Dad's was the picture Miel made of the Rockall capture, my most favorite of all would be the canvas of that friend of Scott's.

Scott teaches English poetry at New York University. Jose Fernandez, though, is a doctor and the nephew of the writer Aurora de Albornoz. Aurora had to flee Spain for Puerto Rico after the war.

When he showed me their library, Jose handed me the piece he prizes most of all. It was a letter of Neruda's, addressed to the poet Gabriel Celaya. The letter was affectionate. At the end Don Pablo says to Celaya that it could turn out they wouldn't see one another again but it didn't matter. They'd see each other every time a Chilean and a Basque met up.

There were a number of us who'd come to the party, most all writers. Among them were the N.Y.U. poetry professor Mark Rudman and the poets Marie Ponsot and Phillis Levin and the Czech filmmaker Vojtech Jasny.

Mark was talking to me about his wife, saying she wasn't part of the literary world, but instead a mathematician. "We get along great, she has what I haven't got and vice versa." I smiled at him, before I laid out how Nerea, too, works with numbers. Then I told him how she works in a bank, and how one customer would come in to see her every so often, and hand her a slip of paper with old words on it. "It's been ages since I've heard this word," he'd say and tell Nerea to put it away somewhere. A retired fisherman regularly gives her words, sayings, the names of fish. He deposits antique words safe in the same place they keep the money in.

The poet Marie Ponsot didn't say too much, she kept quiet listening to the rest of us. When she did talk, anyhow, she tended to speak a sentence of the kind you remember forever.

Marie is advanced in age. In her youth she went to France and married there, though a few years afterward the couple returned to New York. Her husband from the beginning had told her he wanted children, she said, and she had said no.

She didn't want to be a mother. She'd never for a second felt that need in herself. She thought she would lose her freedom. Even during the time she was pregnant she hadn't felt anything particularly special. But when her daughter came out of her belly and she saw that face, she felt then what she hadn't felt ever before: that she was at one with the world.

Jose confessed to us, among friends and after downing a few cosmopolitans, that he'd like to make a trip to Spain and get married there, in his aunt Aurora's birthplace. Scott, however, was of a different opinion. Even though marriage between same-sex couples was legal in Spain he preferred to go on the way they'd been.

The talk turned to same-sex adoption. Apropos of that I told them about what had happened to this one man in Ondarroa who trained songbirds. Olea was known for his songbirds and had won a number of prizes, too, around Biscay, with these birds. He was in the custom, on top of that, of giving his birds the names of Basque troubadours.

He once took it into his head to breed a female blackbird with a male song thrush. Something nobody had done before. In no time at all word spread throughout the town and a lot of people went to pay Olea a visit, asking if the blackbird had laid an egg yet by any chance. Nevertheless, things weren't going as well as people thought they were. As to getting along, the birds got along together all right but the blackbird laid no eggs. The days passed, spring progressed and still no sign of an egg.

One fine day, some astute visitor realised that this blackbird wasn't a female, but a male instead. Both blackbird and song thrush were male birds.

Olea couldn't accept the fact of his blunder. How was it possible for the most famous bird trainer around not to know the difference between a male and a female blackbird?

Then they had the notion of putting a cuckoo's egg in the cage, since they knew for a fact that a cuckoo egg thrives in any bird's nest. And so it was that the little cuckoo hatched, there in the nest of the song thrush and the blackbird.

Scott proposed a toast to Olea's memory. Cosmopolitans were raised on high. Vojtech Jasny recorded the scene with his camera. Jasny is in the habit of filming his life. This eighty-two-year-old Czech filmmaker is in the process of making a documentary of his life, which is going to be as long as the life itself. Like that map Borges mentions, the most perfect of all maps. So perfect that it's the size of the world.

The party finished up. As we were saying our goodbyes, Vojtech spoke a single sentence to me: "Nothing happens for nothing."

Anything can spark a memory. Smells, for instance. The smell of a cleaning fluid. When we used to go see Dad in the

I.C.U. there was always the same smell, the smell of a cleaning fluid. After a bunch of years had gone by, I got a whiff of the same smell when I went into the toilet of a restaurant in Bilbao. At that moment, a sentence suddenly came into my mind. "It's not worth operating all over again." What the surgeon said. When he flung that harsh sentence at us, I'd been breathing that cleaning-fluid smell.

On September 21st they were going to run a test on Dad. He'd spent nine days in the I.C.U. already. Since we went to see him every single day, it seemed the gravity of his situation escaped our minds. We saw him, a few short days after the heart operation and critical care, going back down to the wards. Dad, however, was still installed right where he was, no way forward, no way back. And that was what worried the doctors.

Illnesses that don't get better end up getting worse.

The test was easy: He had to eat a yogurt. Until then he'd had no solid food. If he ate the yogurt and the pancreas responded favorably, the doctors told him, he could move down to the wards the following day. He was full of hope.

The following day, though, they called home from the hospital. His pancreas had begun to hemorrhage. They'd need him to undergo an operation. A life-or-death one.

Mother and Aunt Margarita hugged him goodbye on the way to the operating theatre, telling him everything would come out fine. When the staff put him on the gurney the three of them sang the children's song "Mother St. Ines," the one you sing to children so they don't have bad dreams.

> Mother St. Ines
> I had a dream last night.
> If it is good,
> we'll wish for it twice.
> If it is bad,
> please put it to flight.

He didn't wake up again.

I've dreamt about my father only once since he's been gone. It wasn't long after he died. He died on October 28, 1999, a south-wind day, after being asleep for a month.

In the dream I was on my way down to the harbor, as usual, to meet him. The way we did every time the *Toki-Argia* was on its way in. But as I went along the wharf looking for the boat, something inside me was telling me this harbor wasn't the everyday one, it had something strange about it, because it was a dream one.

All at once, I did find Dad. He was alongside the *Toki-Argia,* pacing nervously. When he saw me he went calm.

"Are all of you all right?" he asked me, concerned. He seemed to be worried, because he'd left us all by ourselves.

"Yes, we're all O.K.," I answered him.

He took a deep breath. Then, we hugged and he climbed onto the boat. It was a long, long hug.

That's where the dream ended. Since then he hasn't reappeared in my dreams. That hug was our goodbye, the one we didn't give each other when he was alive.

18

THE MAN FROM STORNOWAY

In New York's Museum of Modern Art hang paintings of Picasso's by the dozens, one after another. The most striking, without a doubt, is the renowned "Les Demoiselles d'Avignon." Picasso painted it in 1907, and it has its origins in a whorehouse on Avinyó Street in Barcelona. The loose-living women of the place appear in the picture. When Picasso painted it he was only twenty-five, and in the canvas you can see how some of the faces have been painted over, that he later turned what had been a man into a woman. Picasso's work has tremendous power, it grabs the viewer from the get-go.

Directly across from the picture are two other paintings, to all appearances both exactly the same. One is a picture of Georges Braque's, titled "Man with a Guitar," and the other is a picture of Picasso's, "Ma Jolie." You almost can't tell whose is one's and whose is the other's. They're from the same period and it looks as if the same hand had painted them both. Both artists were delving into the possibilities of Cubism and both came out with the same picture. We don't know which of them based his picture on the other's.

But those two works finally say little or nothing to the viewer, they're cold, dark. A technique has been taken to its extreme, that's all they demonstrate.

I turn and look once again at the painting of Picasso's youth. Those "demoiselles" do keep something in reserve. Picasso wanted to throw open the curtain and show what was behind it, something unexpected. And even now a viewer registers the surprise. It's not a technically perfect painting, and at the beginning they criticised it for that, Matisse himself took it as an insult to modern art. But it's intensely alive.

And when you look at the picture you know at first sight that it's Picasso's – not "Ma Jolie," though. It could be either Picasso's or Braque's.

Maybe it was for that very reason that Picasso diverged from the path of extreme Cubism and began painting different pictures, more colourful ones, livelier ones. He used to say that that path had come to a dead end because after the First World War people didn't want to see dark things, people needed joy in life. And people took up Picasso as their own.

I remember how when I was little we, too, had a copy of the "Guernica" picture hanging in the living room. There would have been a "Guernica" in every house in the Basque Country at the time. Our parents put a coat of varnish on it and it looked like the painting was real. I remember I thought the real "Guernica" was in our house and the ones I saw in my friends' houses were nothing but copies of the one in our house.

I even had a set-to with a friend at school, over whether that was so or not. I finally had to accept that the one in our house was like the others, except with a coat of varnish on it.

But it's also the truth that a little bit of varnish is sometimes enough to make things real, a small detail enough to make things different.

That's exactly what Picasso did.

Our dad liked for us to go crazy when he came in from sea. Even when it was bedtime too. He'd sit down on the bed beside us and tell us stories he made up himself. For instance, he'd tell us that when he went to sea he wasn't going to work, he had another wife in a town called Stornoway and four children, too, just like us, and he went off to be with them. I didn't get a wink of sleep, trying to imagine what that other family of Dad's must be like, what they'd look like.

Stornoway is the capital of the Isle of Lewis, in northern Scotland. Mum had the dream of getting to that port at some time or another, that port Dad used to go on about so often.

A small prop plane took us all there, in July of this year. By air it's an hour's trip from Edinburgh. When the aircraft was making its descent for landing you could see green meadows from the window, peat bogs, not a single tree.

Despite its being July foul weather welcomed us. Wind and rain. At the first fine chance we went down to the harbor. That before anything else. The port of Stornoway is built in a sheltered natural harbor. At the outer wharf ferries and naval vessels were moored, the fishing boats on the inward side. There must have been a half dozen tied up at dock then. Their names struck us, because they were very optimistic. The boats were called *Good Luck, Great Fishing* and names like that. I immediately thought of the name of our dad's boat, *Toki-Argia* – the Bright-Spot. That itself was not such an appropriate name for a boat that worked off Rockall.

Our hotel was also right by the port, a residence called the Thorlee Guest House. When we got there, though, there wasn't a soul around. We rang the bell and nobody stirred.

At some point, we saw that there were hotel cards on a small table by the front door. We called the number on the card and the proprietor picked up. "Uribe. We've been waiting on you," he came out with to my amazement. He said that since it was Sunday they'd gone to the pictures and the keys were in the drawer of the table by the front door. There'd be no supper in the hotel but not to worry ourselves, the best we could do would be to have our supper at the restaurant of the Royal Hotel.

We had a single task in Stornoway. We were on the track of a man named Angus MacLeod. The lawyer Isidor Etxebarria had told us to talk with him. That Angus MacLeod would know of the doings of that era, since he'd been the harbormaster of Stornoway port.

We had only a slip of paper that said "Angus MacLeod, Amity House" on it.

The next day, we asked the hotel man if he knew anyone by the name of Angus MacLeod. He replied that, around that town, Angus MacLeod could be anyone at all, since the given name was common and the surname more so. He was right, the petrol station was "MacLeod's," and so was the perfume shop. Anyhow, once he heard "Amity House" he suggested we go down by the harbor, that house was right there, and ask the people of the place.

We found the building just where he said we would. A woman answered our knock and asked us in. At the mention of Angus's name she gave us a smile. "He's taken his retirement." Then we told her that Isidor Etxebarria had sent us there, that we came from the Basque Country and our father had worked on a boat called the *Toki-Argia.*

When the woman, standing in front of us, called him on the phone, Angus said yes right away. "He's walking the dog," the woman told us, "but at half-twelve he'll be waiting for you at the sailors' aid home."

When we reached the sailors' aid home there was Angus, chatting with a few other aid workers at the front door. As soon as he saw us he greeted us as if we were old friends. In a leap and a bound he led us to his office on the second floor. The man was up in years but physically was in great shape. Going up the stairs we found photographs of vessels that had been saved since the end of the nineteenth century. There were Basque boats, too, the *St. Michael of Arretxinaga* and the *Gaztelubide*. The latter was shipwrecked on December 18, 1970. From that dragger they rescued fourteen people.

Angus told us he'd been stunned once, watching television, when a restaurant suddenly appeared called Gaztelubide. He'd assumed the place was kin with the boat and had thought, I'd eat there myself with pleasure. We explained to him it wasn't truly a restaurant, but instead a gastronomical society.

Apropos eating he recalled another thing that had happened, how once because their radio was broken a Basque boat requested their help. When they drew up in the inflatable tender, they invited them to eat by way of thanks. "We ate pig's feet and lamb-tripe sausages, *tripotxak,* would've raised a dead man." The food those fishermen cooked up was apparently so delicious that they'd all kept yearning for the moment that boat would get into some kind of distress, for her to return once again to Stornoway harbor, and them to get a taste of those glorious pig's feet.

Angus well remembered the names of the boats that twenty years earlier had worked around Rockall, he rattled off the whole list for us. "Those were very good years, uncommon lively." It seemed as if the man hadn't in fact been walking his dog that morning, but instead been going through old papers, the better to prepare for the conversation he'd be having with us. "Each time we hauled them in, the whole throng of them came in saying they hadn't done a thing, they hadn't known they were in Scottish waters. The Basques were good men, at one time twenty launches or upward, too, were moored in Stornoway harbor. There was never once any quarrel with them. They generated a good atmosphere in the pubs. Whenever the English came in, aye, then there'd be some whopping fights."

Angus was bedazzled by those fishermen who came from southern Europe. "They knew how to catch good-quality fish. But it was stunning how they worked, in a very simple manner. They used stone blocks and such to send the nets to the bottom. They bore no resemblance whatever to the factory ships come out of Germany or Denmark. The Basques didn't need any great contraption to catch fish with. With a net, enough and to spare."

Angus's dream was to get to know the Cantabrian coast. At least that's what he confessed to us. His wife was ill, in a depression, he said, but if she snapped out of it they'd make an excursion to the Basque Country.

The situation was weird. Dad's alleged enemy, that man who'd taken Basque boats in under guard, now desired to go to the Basque Country. As we had gone to get to know Stornoway, he wanted to get to know our home place.

The night before, we'd had supper at the Royal Hotel as the fellow at the inn had said to. Grilled monkfish. At the end of the meal, Mum gave us a surprise. She read us some passages from her diary. She's been writing a daily journal ever since our dad's been gone. She tells him all the things that have happened in the family since then. "Don't look at me like that. It's as easy as writing a letter," she'd said nine years earlier when she told us of her intention. She went up to Arantzazu all by herself and there began keeping her diary, in the year 2000.

At supper, she read us the first pages out loud. She'd written in our local dialect and somehow sounded just as she'd used to when speaking to him at home.

> "If I didn't do this very thing I'd have no peace
> whatever – I've been looking for you all over
> the place and right here is where I expect I'll

find you. How will I look for you, though, if I myself don't know where I've gone missing? First I'll find you and then find myself, since I really do feel I've been cut in two.

"Well, Jose, I'm not up to writing, either, and so till tomorrow. I've always loved you and that's how I'll go on until I die, you were my first and by all the looks of it my last.

"Till tomorrow,
             Antigua"

As for that other family of Dad's I have to say, we didn't find anyone at all who looked anything like us.

Unai likes soccer. He plays on the town team in the teen league. Left wing midfielder. On PlayStation there's a soccer game, and he spends hours and hours with it. The game reflects the usual functioning of a soccer team. There are championships, and once the championship is over there's the chance to sign players. All the teams in Europe are in the PlayStation game, all the soccer players in Europe. When you play this game you have to choose a team and use it to play with.

He always picks Chelsea. He says Chelsea is his favorite, he's a Chelsea fan. That grieves me. How he's not a follower of any of the Basque teams, or of the one with all Basque players. "When I was your age I was an Athletic fan," I sometimes say to him, engaging in some emotional blackmail. "But Athletic always loses," he complains. "I'd rather be a Chelsea fan and win the Champions League." I leave his room feeling downcast.

Today, too, I went into his room and found him on the PlayStation. "I've got good news for you," he said to me with a grin. "I'm playing with Athletic and we're in a position to win the Champions League!" I couldn't contain my joy. Finally the boy is on the right track, I said to myself. But at some point I realised that one of his Athletic players was black. "Who is that?" I asked. "I don't know him." "That's Drogba, the Chelsea forward. I signed him for the Athletic Club," he replied. "And I got Torres and Messi too. Athletic is the best team in the world now."

It's clear as day, there's nothing to be done with this boy.

19

MONTREAL

Distance to Destination: 785 miles
Time to destination: 1:41 hours
Local Time: 05:37 PM
Ground Speed: 520 mph
Altitude: 36,700
Outside air temperature: -67° F
Halifax, Chicoutimi, Montreux

The flight attendants' bustling to and fro wakes me. They're getting breakfast. Renata is still asleep. I go down the stairs to the toilet. The toilets are to either side, and straight in front of me is a big mirror. I see my face in it. I've gotten more rest than I thought. The door of one of the toilets opens, Little Miss Sunshine and her mother come out. The child stands staring at me. Her mother yanks at her arm and takes her up the stairs.

I go back to my seat. Idly I take up the Lufthansa magazine. Settle in to look at the products for sale. Perfumes. Calvin Klein. ONE. 39 Euros / 13,500 points. Issey Miyake. L'eau d'Issey pour homme. 57 Euros / 17,000 points.

When I get to the watches, on page 46, one ad catches my eye.

Skagen Watch Leather Slimline
NEW

99 Euros / 30,000 miles.

> Ultraslim stainless steel watch integrated top-quality leather strap. Sophisticated sleek and timeless Danish design from Skagen. 3 year warranty on quartz movement. Mineral Crystal. 3 atm. Size: 0134.1mm.

Skagen, the Danish cape where the North Sea and the Baltic meet, is known for two things. For one, the designer watches of the same name. The other is the school of painting people brought into being there around 1900. There was a special light on those beaches where the two seas become one and the painters headed out to record that in their pictures. Michael Ancher, Ana Ancher and P. S. Krøyer. In a book about those painters, I found this story:

Skagen was known for its shipwrecks. It was believed the inhabitants lit small fires to cause wrecks on the reefs. The captain of a freighter would think those fires were the lights of houses, and would make in to the coast. That would be their downfall. The vessels would hit the reefs and founder.

The inhabitants of Skagen profited by those shipwrecks to get raw materials for themselves.

The magistrate Ole Christian Lund left the life of the capital city of Copenhagen and retired up there to Skagen. At the start of the nineteenth century, in 1803 to be more precise. He bought some land beside the sea, ten hectares of land, and there he planted some fast-growing trees. Elms, poplars and willows.

One night, he took into his home a man who'd been shipwrecked. Somebody knocked on his door in the dead of night, imploring him to look after this man who was surely near his end. The shipwrecked sailor was from the United States, the captain of a freighter running out of South Carolina. The vessel was taking cotton and rice into the Baltic.

When the man had revived, Lund took him out to see his trees. And explained how he looked after them. In one of their conversations, he showed the captain a cotton boll he'd found on the beach when the shipwreck took place, and asked him how the plant was cultivated. The captain told him that in the temperate lands of the Southern United States the cotton plantations were gigantic, and picking it was backbreaking work, black slaves who'd come from Africa did it.

Once he'd fully recovered, the captain set out on his way back to the land of his birth. When they said their goodbyes he asked Magistrate Lund how he could repay him for saving his life, he'd be in his debt as long as he lived.

"One of those Southern slaves'll do me no harm. I'm too old to be managing all this land on my own," the Magistrate apparently said to him half kidding, half not. The captain gave him a grin and was lost from view down the cart track.

Magistrate Ole Christian Lund had forgotten all about his conversation with the captain when, one morning, he saw a small three-masted sloop out at sea. From the sailboat they lowered a skiff into the water, and four men rowed it ashore, two oarsmen on either side. In its prow a man with a broad-brimmed hat, standing erect. You could tell the man was carrying something or other on his shoulder.

Once Ole Christian Lund got down to the beach he realised that the man was black.

"I am your payment for having saved the captain's life," the man said to him as soon as they'd greeted each other. Ole Christian could not believe it, the American captain had sent him a slave. "Herewith the slave Jan from South Carolina in the United States of America," it said in the short letter he'd brought with him.

They called the first black man ever seen in that territory Jan Leton. For the local people Leton was the devil himself.

And that belief spread throughout the township. That thing he carried on his shoulder was a monkey, Jocko, also a gift from the captain.

The Magistrate took Leton in gladly, considered him a freedman and they worked together pruning the trees. In town, on the contrary, they didn't take to him at all. He was the equal of pigs as far as they were concerned. The local fishermen didn't give him the time of day. If he went to the tavern and wanted someone to talk with, he himself had to stand a round for the house.

He died in 1827, at the age of 56. A year before the Magistrate. In Skagen they say that when he died they didn't bury him in the graveyard. The body of that "devil" had to lie in unconsecrated ground. And for that reason they buried him between the two largest dunes on the beach.

That's what they say in the town, but the tale has little truth to it. At least if we refer back to the church papers. In the documents you see clear as anything that they put Leton in his grave according to the Christian rite.

And so the story of their burying him among the dunes has no foundation in fact. But where did the story of the dunes come from? Was it pure fantasy? Why are the townspeople so sure Jan's remains lie on the beach?

That burial in the dunes was only a lapse of memory. More unequivocably, a confusion impelled into being by

Jan's alleged devil essence. In fact, what's buried among the dunes is not Jan Leton, the first black man to reach Skagen. Who rests between the two largest dunes is somebody else: Jocko the playful monkey. And thence the mixup.

On Ole Christian Lund's land, nowadays, there's a large park and a lot of visitors go there on the weekends, to enjoy the peace of Lund's trees.

The Rockall fishing ground was called the 56th Bank. Between the rocky outcrop of Rockall and the Isles of St. Kilda. That's where the draggers started fishing in 1979. When asked what kind of years those ones at Rockall had been, the old captains Leon Ituarte and Pako Uranga said "Good," savoring the word. I had a date to meet up with them in the port of Mutriku, in August. Leon had worked for the same company as our dad, but on another boat, called the *Toki-Alai*. Pako, though, had been on the *Legorpe*.

At the beginning only three or four boats went up there, as a rule. There was no chart of the fishing ground either. There were only sea-route charts, but nobody knew where the banks were, where the reefs were or the fish. They had to make all the maps themselves. Even I remember how Dad made his charts at home, the depths of that sea terrain he imagined in blue, red and black marking pens.

"Fishing, your dad was one of the best, but he was a born liar too." At that time when only three or four boats were working, they'd leave the radios on from eight in the morning to six in the evening. Saying how any boat's fishing was going, though, was another matter.

"Your dad was a sly one. He was such a liar that one time all the rest of us thought of not saying boo to him over the radio, when he'd ask us we'd just keep mum. We weren't going to give away our heading to that one," Pako told me.

When our dad turned on the radio as usual and asked after their situation no one told him a thing. "But he was a wheedler, suave, and right away he pried the state of affairs out of Leon. He knew how to talk." Their revenge went no farther than that.

"However, if you really want the whole story, he was a born seaman. Once, off the coast of France a big wave hit a boat and took her bridge out. The bridge and the captain vanished into the sea. There was the boat, no radio, no radio-beacon buoy, adrift. Your dad found her and got the news to the rescue service," Pako declared.

That radio business brought me a memory from when we were little. Dad had a game he played with us. He'd call in on the radio and tell us he'd caught some fish. In such a way that everyone could listen to it, since out at sea some one or another of the captains would be listening in.

Dad would use a code. Only he and us knew that code. It was easy as could be. For instance, he'd write these words on paper:

FIDELCASTRO

Then, beneath each letter he'd put the number of boxes of the catch from small to large. Under the letter **F** he put 1,000, under the letter **I** 1,100, under the **D** 1,200. And so on until it got to 2,000 boxes for the **O**.

"Dad, how's the fishing going?" we'd ask and if he said "Orio" how thrilled we kids would be. The boat was coming in jam-packed with two thousand boxes of fish.

Everything had to be invented at Rockall. They went there with the nets they used on the Gran Sol fishery, but those were no use. They were speedily full of holes. The men would cut strands from the ends of ropes and tie these one by one to a net's underside. That way they didn't tear through so fast. That to catch sand dab, pollack and monkfish. To catch scorpion fish, however, you had to go where the coral was and there you had no way out. It always tore you full of holes. It occurred to one of the captains to insert ball bearings into the bag, so the back of the net would lift up and not get holes in it. "Always that was the notion. True, when we came ashore we would realise this fellow or that one was using that selfsame gear. To us, out there, none of them were saying. Once we came ashore, all our nets torn up, then we realised what the old captains were using in the way of tricks."

The old charts of that time don't answer these days. Captains nowadays have CD maps onscreen and there's where the undersea banks show up. But no fish show up anywhere at all there. "For fish Rockall's no breeding ground. They go through there. Fish have the same movements birds do, they migrate the way they do. We knew each season of the year, and even each day, what fish would be passing through there. March, for one example, is the season for monkfish. But now the habits have gone and changed. On the seabed out there there's nothing, except our own old ropes." In the best of those years twenty boats went to Rockall out of Ondarroa, now only two. The *Legorpe* and the *Kirriski*, they're the last.

The Rockall seas are rough, the southwest is the worst. You work from morning to nightfall. But there are other moments too. Pako told how once he came back to town with a broken leg. But the accident hadn't been work-related. They came into port in Ireland. The whole crew got into a soccer game against the Irish kids. He didn't tell me who won, the fishermen or the Irish. He didn't remember. That he'd come back with a broken leg, he had that clear enough.

"A boat that's steady in the water catches the most fish. She has to squat down in the water, sturdy. That's why your ballast is important. The more weight, the more fish. If her prow is higher than her stern, or vice versa, there's no fishing. People are like that too. A person's got to be steady on his pins. And so does a boat. Otherwise there's no catching fish." That's what Leon said. I recalled the book I'm writing, you need security in order to write. Absence of fear. "If you scare easy, don't ever go to sea."

The way the conversation ended touched me deeply. Pako, as we were about to say goodbye, began listing the names of the captains who were active in those beginning years, as if it were the lineup of a soccer team, as if they were soldiers who had gone off to a war together. He spoke the names one by one. "Justo Larrinaga. Jose Uribe. Agustin Agirregomezkorta. Leon Ituarte. Pako Uranga. Joakin Urkiza. Juan Mari Zelaia. Luciano Paz . . . There we all were, way off there."

The news of ETA's last ceasefire caught me in Madrid on March 24, 2006. A friend called me on my mobile. He was overjoyed, "What we've been hoping for years on end has finally happened" was what he said.

When I answered my mobile I was standing in the Madrid headquarters of the BBVA (the onetime Bank of Bilbao).

Looking at Arteta's murals, to be precise. They looked to me to have aged, and I was the only person in the circular room who was looking at the paintings. Executives strode through coming and going, in a hurry, their heads obviously full of several other things.

That coincidence, to be standing looking at those murals on the day of the ceasefire, in Bastida's building, was glorious.

I remembered then the kindness Aurelio Arteta himself and the Arrue brothers had shown to Tomas Meabe. Meabe was on his deathbed in Madrid, penniless and stricken with tuberculosis. Arteta and the Arrues sold their pictures to help Meabe out with some money in that difficult situation. They all held different ideological beliefs but admired one another.

I also recalled that saying of Aunt Maritxu's, about the people Grandmother Ana had in her home during the war. "Ideas are one thing and the heart is another." I had thought for a long time that Aunt Maritxu was wrong. The saying was too lovely for wartime. Money would have more to do with taking in lodgers than the heart would. But I was the one who wasn't right. That day, if only for a moment, Aunt's saying took on its full meaning, the heart won out over ideas.

One rainy November day a skinny little fellow got out of an elegant black car on Commandant Velarde Street, across from the house Liborio Uribe had lived in. As he got out of the car he stepped in a puddle and soiled his suit. They'd taken up the old paving stones to maintain the street a bit and what with the rain the whole neighbourhood had turned into a swamp. Jose Luis Meler had come from Bilbao to pay a final farewell to the old friend who'd saved his life in the escape from Larrinaga jail.

Liborio died of a throat tumor after a long deathwatch. In the nights the fear of death would come over him and he'd ask our father to sleep beside him, in his room. A few hours later, when Granddad fell asleep, Dad would creep silently out of the room and go to the room where Mum was sleeping. After all, they were newlyweds. But a bit afterwards Granddad would wake up in a fright and be calling for Dad. Our father would get out of bed and go to our grandfather, to calm him down, until he fell back to sleep.

All during those long days when Liborio was bedridden our Grandma Anparo, his fellow in-law, would come to visit him. Even though Anparo was an ardent Basque nationalist, she'd sit at Liborio's bedside every afternoon and read him the Francoist press. I can imagine Grandma's way of reading, like that of a child, slow, stressing each syllable. Every once in a while, Anparo would quit reading and light into Liborio: "What lies your friends tell. This is the last time I'm reading you this nonsense." Liborio would smile at her with his eyes. He knew for certain Anparo was kidding. He knew for certain that the next afternoon, too, Anparo would come to visit him and read him the newspaper.

They buried Liborio on that rainy November day. Jose Luis Meler paid all the funeral expenses.

20

BOSTON

Distance to Destination: 195 miles
Time to destination: 0:33 hours
Local Time: 06:40 PM
Ground Speed: 516 mph
Altitude: 34,000
Outside air temperature: -47° F
Boston, Fall River, Hartford

We're passing over Boston. In the spring of 2007 I had a reading in Cambridge with Elizabeth. We read the poems in Basque and in English. It was weird to see the college students taking notes during the reading. Since we were in Cambridge, Elizabeth took me to see the glass flowers at Harvard University.

In 1886, George Lincoln Goodale, the director of the Harvard Botanical Museum, set out for Dresden. Something was worrying him. When he taught botany classes they used dried plant specimens and they didn't show the beauty of the plants. Replicas were made in papier-mâché or photographically, too, but they didn't fill the bill the way they should have. Goodale wanted something else.

He knew there was a family of artisans in Germany who made replicas of invertebrates. That was the objective of his trip, to talk with the Blaschka glassworking family.

Leopold and Rudolf, father and son, listened to his proposal. Goodale saw some plants made of glasswork in the artisans' home and that increased his hopes.

They told him no. They had enough work with the invertebrates, and the father moreover foresaw many dilemmas in making the plants. He'd tried doing it long ago and it always turned out badly. He'd made these replicas because he'd felt like it, and then had sold almost all of them to a Belgian museum, but he had bad memories of that transaction. He sold them for very little and shortly afterward the museum itself burned down, in a fire.

But Goodale didn't give up, he persisted, plants like those were absolutely essential for the further advancement of science. Seeing his passion, the Blaschkas promised him that they would make three or four replicas, as an experiment.

When they'd finished, they sent the replicas off to the United States by mail. Unfortunately, at Customs they opened the crate and those glass flowers shattered into seven thousand pieces. Nevertheless, they were so beautiful, Blaschka and his son had done such fine work, that everyone at the university who saw the shards of the flowers accepted that this was the way to go, the beauty of flowers was best reflected in glass.

Elizabeth C. Ware and her daughter Mary Lee were bedazzled by the plants. Entirely astounded. And they begged Dr. Goodale to get as many such replicas as he could, to sign a contract with the Germans as soon as possible and if money was by any chance a problem they themselves would put up the necessary cash.

The Blaschkas said yes to the proposal that came from Harvard. True, they made one thing clear. They would be working half days on the plants, since they needed the other half day to fill the orders of earlier clients.

They didn't have much time, and had to start work as quickly as possible. The first task, choosing the species.

The seeds of plants on the list of the chosen were sent from the United States to Germany, to be cultivated and used as models. But not all of them. There were numerous plants, exotics and tropical plants for instance, that were easy to come by neither in Germany nor at Harvard. Leopold Blaschka learned that such plants were grown in the garden of the park of the Saxon princes' Schloss Pillnitz. These plants were secret, so that only the royal family had the pleasure of their beauty. Leopold Blaschka, nonetheless, managed to be granted permission.

In April of 1887 they sent the first twenty samples to the United States. Because of the bad experience they'd had with Customs before, they requested that the boxes be opened right there at the University, in front of a Customs worker. The authorities did give their approval.

The Blaschkas certainly knew how to send the plants. With wire they fastened each model to a cardboard foundation, and wrapped the more delicate parts in tissue paper. Then, each one was put into a cardboard box. When several boxes were ready, they put them into a large wooden crate, stuffing straw between the boxes. That way the cardboard boxes wouldn't knock against each other, or against the wood of the crate. Finally, the large wooden crate was sealed shut, and they enclosed the whole of it in a large cloth pouch. The package was now as tall as a person.

When three years had passed they realised the work was going very slowly and instead of working half days they determined to work full time. On April 16, 1890, the Blaschkas and Goodale signed the new contract. They'd have to complete the work in ten years and would be unable to take on any other jobs. They had to send the plants to America twice a year, with Harvard paying all expenditures.

In 1895 while Rudolf Blaschka was in Jamaica acquainting himself with tropical plants close-up, his father, Leopold, died. The son would have to face the work that remained to be done all by himself. He completed the job in 1936.

There had been a lot of rumours at one time about the process by which these plants were made. On the subject, Leopold Blaschka wrote this: "Many think we have some sort of machine that creates the plants. But that's not the way it is, our secret is the sense of touch. Rudolf has it more than I do, because the sense of touch increases from generation to generation. The only way to be a virtuoso in glassworking is this: to have a great-grandfather who loves glass, for that great-grandfather to have a son who takes pleasure in glass, and for that one's son as well to be a great aficionado of glass in turn. Finally you yourself as their offspring have to gain your mastery and receive that inheritance and if you have no success it is entirely your own fault. But if you have no forebears, you're working in vain. My grandfather was the best-known crystal-maker in Bohemia and he lived for eighty-three years. My own father too, comparable. And I, too, would like my hands not to tremble until I'm that age."

There was no other secret at all.

Nowadays these glass plants are on display at the Harvard Museum of Natural History, in glass cases. Even looking at them close-up, you can't tell whether they're glass or are real.

I told Nerea about the miracle of the flowers at Harvard. "They're glorious," she said to me, "but they have a flaw. They don't smell like anything."

Renata wakes up and takes off her headphones. You can hear an opera playing from them, Mozart's *Figaro*.

> *Parlo d'amor vegliando,*
> *parlo d'amor sognando,*
> *all'acqua, all'ombre, ai monti,*
> *ai fiori, all'erbe, ai fonti,*
> *all'eco, all'aria, ai venti,*
> *che il suon de' vani accenti*
> *portano via con sé.*
> *E se non ho chi mi oda,*
> *parlo d'amor con me.*

The flight attendants are distributing some papers. Renata takes only one. They've given me two documents with a number of questions. One's green, for the visa, and the other white, for Customs.

"I had a glorious sleep," Renata says to me after swallowing some coffee. "We've got barely an hour till we get in."

"I found it shorter than I thought, too, talking's helpful that way."

"True. And from when we were first talking, I've got a question pending that I'd like to ask you. Did you ever manage to find out who the second friend of the *Dos Amigos* was?"

"You're going to laugh when you hear. In the end it wasn't that important."

Among the questions they ask on the green paper, they request the address I'll be staying at in the United States. "10 Columbus Circle. Apartment 12C. New York, NY 10019." It's Karmentxu Pascual's house.

Karmentxu left home when she was fourteen. Left Donostia–San Sebastián and went to New York along with her mother. In that bitter decade of the nineteen-fifties. They had an aunt waiting for them there, a seamstress. The aunt was said to make clothes for Jose Antonio Agirre and Jesus Galindez of the Basque government-in-exile. Fourteen years old when she went and even today living in the Americas.

When I'm staying at her house we have breakfast together every day. From the window you can see the New York streets. Cars and people, in their ebb and flow. Karmen lives alone. Her children are grown, each of them making a life of their own.

"No one greets you on the street here," she said to me once as we ate breakfast, and added, "That's normal, in a city like this you never meet up with the same person twice on the street." Karmen makes her living as an interpreter. When she retires she wants to move back to Donostia, she told me.

In fact, even though she's been living in New York she hasn't forgotten her hometown. "Lately I've been walking around like Martin of Igaraburu's donkey, with blinders on," she'll say when she makes a mistake.

She wants to move back to Donostia and take up a long-term plan she's had, to learn Basque in fact. She does know a few words in Basque, among them one she repeats time and again, *goxua* – sweet, soothing, delicious, gentle, a delight. She's always remembered that one word. In her opinion that's what's most important in life, the state or condition resulting from *goxua*.

I found out that I knew nothing of the mystery behind the name *Dos Amigos*. We made a date to go out fishing with Uncle Santi and Uncle Txomin, our dad's brothers. We boarded their boat, a vessel called *Amu Ezpanin* (Hook in the Lip), and made for Lekeitio, to an inlet called Sagustan. When we came even with Irabaltza Rock Uncle cut the engines.

"Here's your granddad's whiting-pout hole, he showed us the way here, but don't you go telling anyone around here later – it's a family secret."

Both uncles are master fishermen, when they were young men they took two inshore boats and made their way from Ondarroa to Venezuela. Santi captained the *Sagustan* and Txomin the *Villa de Ondarroa*. One went before and the other close behind. When I asked how they got to the Caribbean, Santi told us they made it there by watching the stars, and paying attention to what Columbus had written. They, too, followed the trade winds from the Canary Islands to Cuba.

They had a contract to fish in Venezuela, but with one condition, they had to buy their bait in Venezuela. However, in their opinion that bait wasn't much good and they decided to catch small fish and use them instead.

They wound up their work and went to sleep. Uncle Santi woke with a gun to his belly. He opened his eyes and a military man stood beside his bunk. They took them prisoner and set out for port. On their way, however, they saw a dragger off in the distance. It was Italian. Leaving the Basques in peace, the Venezuelan military men took off after the Italians. In fact, they preferred catching big fish to catching little ones.

They also told me other stories. This, for example, which Uncle Txomin had heard from a friend.

Bilbao. The nineteen-sixties. The dictator's going to be paying a visit to the city. They've readied all the streets, ordered every one spruced up, sent all idlers and beggars out of town. The news of Franco's visit reaches the jail too. And they've prepared a film as well, heralding the visit, to show to the prisoners. The authorities want to make perfectly clear that Franco no longer has any enemies, and where but in Bilbao, the city that stood up under the fascists' attack for an entire year. Thousands and thousands of people go out into the streets to greet him.

The prisoners begin watching the film, under orders. Most are sickened. Bilbao isn't what it once was. Every last corner of the city is overflowing with people. They show the scene at the City Hall square. That, too, is full to the brim. The joy in the streets is obvious, everyone's cheering Franco. All of a sudden, a man who's climbed a streetlamp in the square appears in the foreground. The man's hanging from the lamppost with one hand and with the other he's making victory signs, clearly elated.

All the prisoners burst into gales of laughter. They cannot believe it. The man who's up on the streetlamp is one of the prisoners right in that very hall. How can that prisoner be out there greeting Franco if he's in jail? The mystery had a simple solution. Those images were from when Athletic won the Cup. And they'd taken images from the welcome rally they'd thrown for the team in the City Hall square and spliced them in with the dictator's close-ups.

Both uncles put my whiting-pout-catching skills to the test. I happened to haul up two whiting pouts in one cast, but don't think that was because I'm a good fisherman. The uncles split their sides laughing at me, when they saw I'd landed the fish "foul-hooked." The poor whiting pouts were hooked not by the mouth but by the gills. I yanked up on the tackle and that's how I caught them. It was impossible not to catch fish in that hole, the school there was so huge.

I remembered the Harvard flowers and what Leopold Blaschka said about working on them. The sense of touch passed from generation to generation, you couldn't start working in glass from scratch, it was necessary to have generations preceding you in the same undertaking. My uncles were using the knowledge they'd learned from their predecessors. The tradition came from any number of earlier generations. And with a glassworker's sense of touch they knew when a fish would take the hook, and what that fish was like. My hooks, however, rose empty to the boat. I wasn't sensing when the fish nibbled the bait on the hook.

All of a sudden, while they were going on about fish, Uncle Santi made a gesture that for a long time I had totally forgotten. To give an idea of the size of a fish he didn't use the distance between two hands, as is usually done, but instead stretched out his left arm and, with his right index finger, indicated on his arm the size of the fish, the way you show where to slice a loaf of bread. Beginning from the tips of the fingers and indicating the size just around the wristbone.

I imagined that this gesture, too, like that forgotten hand sign Aunt Maritxu made, was on its way to being lost.

At the end of three hours the *Amu Ezpanin* came into port. We divvied up the fish, they took three or four and gave me all the rest for our household.

When we were about to leave the boat Santi came back from the bridge carrying an envelope. "You asked me ages back where that 'Dos Amigos' came from and I had no idea whatever, but I found this here in the old papers."

Uncle handed me a document. On the paper was the history of the *San Agustin*. "San Agustin, SS-3-765." When and where they built the boat, and how it passed from one owner to the other. At first I didn't understand what it was, but then I realised that the *San Agustin* was the *Dos Amigos* and that on this paper was written when and why it had been given that name.

Florentino Urkiaga asked Teodoro Ugalde, shipwright, to build the vessel *San Agustin*. On August 11, 1921, he took title to it, paying 4,000 pesetas. On September 16, 1921, Zezilio Aldarondo bought it from him for 3,500 pesetas. On May 8, 1925, Maria Teresa Arakistain received the vessel as an inheritance. On June 25, 1925, Deograzias Burgoa bought it from her at a price of 2,200 pesetas. On June 25,

1928, Pedro Artetxe and Jose Mari Goiogana bought the vessel *San Agustin* in partnership, for 2,000 pesetas. A month after buying it the new owners changed the name of the *San Agustin,* to christen it the *Dos Amigos.* Finally, on March 10, 1941, Liborio Uribe bought the aged, twenty-year-old *Dos Amigos,* paying 500 pesetas.

So that's what the boat's history said. Our grandfather Liborio had nothing at all to do with the name *Dos Amigos.* The earlier owners had given the boat that name. There was no lost friend, there was no mystery at all.

21

LANDING

> Distance to Destination: 88 miles
> Time to destination: 0:20 hours
> Local Time: 06:54 PM
> Ground Speed: 421 mph
> Altitude: 19,500
> Outside air temperature: -4° F

On the PA system they say the plane will be landing soon. The fasten-seat-belts sign lights up. The passengers take their seats. The flight attendants walk by us to make sure we're strapped in. The aircraft banks and turns.

Two thousand eight. September 21. Saturday night. Four-thirty in the morning. Ondarroa. I've had a bad dream. I'm hanging from the railing of the balcony at my parents' house, in danger of falling. A loud noise wakes me. The house cracks. The jalousies in our room leap inward. There's been a big explosion. I look over at Nerea. She's O.K. "Where's Unai?" I ask her. That's the time he was supposed to be coming home. "Where's Unai?"

The airplane's begun its descent, the wings quake as they cross through the clouds. One of our overhead bins flies open with a bang. The attendant named L. Thompson struggles down the aisle to shut it. She couldn't walk. As if she were on a ship. She almost falls getting the bin shut.

We go to Unai's room. He hasn't come in. His bed is against the window. The glass is shattered. The jalousie mounting and chunks of plaster on his pillow. Nerea calls him on the phone. He picks up right away. He's O.K. He's running late. Thank heavens. I go out on the balcony. Smoke, broken shopwindows, the alarm at the daycare center doesn't shut up.

The turbulence continues. There's a racket inside the aircraft. The flight attendants take their seats. They fasten their seat belts.

Distance to Destination: 69 miles
Time to destination: 0:15 hours
Local Time: 06:57 PM
Ground Speed: 350 mph
Altitude: 13,126
Outside air temperature: 15° F

The People's Guard station house across the river. That's where they've put the bomb. You can hear frightened voices. Calling to each other. "Kepa, Kepa," they're saying. Patrols, ambulances. Little by little the neighbours are coming out into the street. Some have their hands all cut up. They're trying to help each other. More than one is worse off than we are.

Renata looks out the window. You can see the borough of Queens down there. The airplane's flying over ocean. The seas are in a fury. You can see the froth on the waves, the wind is fierce.

I look at the housewife who lives across from me. She's begun picking up the glass. Her husband was killed by right-wing paramilitaries in 1980. He was pro-independence. Her daughter was in my class. We weren't older than ten. That was the first time I was conscious of the grimness of the conflict. Members of the secret police turned up at the funeral. Somebody realised and people confronted them. They lifted a pistol from one of the policemen. They never did find that pistol.

The aircraft wheels earthward. It seems like we're going to fall into the ocean. Renata looks at me. She puts her hand on mine for a moment.

The kids are on their way home from their wild parties, wearing clothing from the Middle Ages. It was a holiday yesterday evening, the anniversary of the founding of the town: 1327, so the six-hundred-and-eighty-first. Today fall began. This fall I'll turn thirty-eight. I've lived the whole of my life with this. Thirty-six years with a conflict and only two or three with some peace. How little.

```
Distance to Destination: 29 miles
Time to destination: 0:09 hours
Local Time: 07:06 PM
Ground Speed: 269 mph
Altitude: 5,422
Outside air temperature: 42° F
```

We see the runway. Gigantic JFK. The jazz-shirt kids want to find skyscrapers by looking out their window. You can't see them. The island of Manhattan is too far away.

There are hunks of metal on the balcony. I go back indoors. I look at my library. The books are on the floor. The ceiling lights dangle. The blast broke the frame of a family photo. Daybreak will arrive. The carpenters will come. They'll replace the jalousies. The television people will pick up and leave. Everything will hardly change at all.

The plane's coming in to land. The camera's back on the screen. The aircraft's little exterior camera, the way it was when we took off. The plane speeds through the clouds. The runway appears. The runway's lines and lights. Ever lower, ever closer. At the moment of landing the camera goes off. On the screen the snow appears.

22

AGIRRE'S ROSES

Resurreccion Maria Azkue was a methodical man. Even when it came time to take his vacation. On the feast day of San Fermin, the seventh of July, he used to go to Lekeitio and in September, right after the Nativity of the Virgin, return to his various duties in Bilbao.

Azkue liked to remain in motion, to go on foot, say, from Lekeitio to Ondarroa, on foot over the mountains. He would enter Ondarroa by the route that comes down from the Antigua hermitage. Right by there was the house where his writer friend Txomin Agirre had been born, on High Street as it happens, the steepest street in town. Azkue and Agirre knew each other well. The one was a linguist and the other a novelist and their relationship dated from their youth, since they'd been schoolmates at the seminary in Gasteiz together.

In Ondarroa people tell how Agirre, despite their close friendship, never asked Azkue into his house. When his friend whistled, Agirre would come out to the street door and there they talked for long stretches, sitting on the stone stoop.

Apparently Agirre was shy about letting Azkue see his parents' poor home, suspecting he might make fun of it.

Azkue was from a good family and Agirre's father was a carpenter. Their house would have been topsy-turvy and better not to put that on display.

In the letters the two of them wrote to each other odd things turn up. For instance, as I mentioned, Azkue was a methodical man and in letters he accuses Agirre of working too little, he's not writing enough.

Agirre's answer tends to be unambiguous. He was abbot at the convent in Zumaia and spent hours and hours all day hearing the nuns' confessions. And after that, he goes on, he's left with little appetite for writing.

He prefers tending the roses in his garden, he says, to sitting down to his quartos to write. For that was Agirre's second love after writing, growing roses. With his roses he was truly at rest, with his roses the world stopped for a moment, and he chased the evil thoughts from his head.

Writing, for Agirre, was work as slow and attentive as caring for his roses.

We Basques have always thought that ours is a small literary tradition. And it's true, if we start counting books published in Basque, there aren't too many. Our literature's had no influence abroad, we've never created a literary work that would be a touchstone, despite having a rich oral tradition.

Among our deficiencies it's often been mentioned that we've had no long epic poem, nothing to equal the great

Chanson de Roland or *Cantar de Mio Cid.* And I'm not talking solely about contemporary stuff, even in the nineteenth century they were retailing those anxieties. And so, toward the middle of the nineteenth century one Garay de Monglave announced to the four corners of the earth that he'd discovered a long epic poem. "The Song of Altabizkar" was the poem. He didn't say that he had made up the poem himself, in 1833, in Paris. Or that he'd written it in French and then asked a student in Bayonne to work it up in Basque.

We don't have any epic poems, it's true. In our literature no one tells the tale of the deeds of a military hero. Inversely, we've got the tale of the wise man, the tale of the one who sold his soul to the devil so as to learn more. In the folk tradition, in the oral stories, the writer Pedro "Axular" Agerre is recalled in exactly that way. The author of the book *Gero* (Later). Our first classic.

In reality Axular studied Art and Theology, in Huesca and in Salamanca, at the end of the sixteenth century. But in the stories it's recounted that in Salamanca he studied in the cavern of the Devil, the way Virgil did in Naples or Faust in Cracow.

It's recounted that, once the school term ended, on Midsummer's Day, all of the students would have to leave the cavern. The Devil made a practice of keeping one student behind with him. They would all form a line to leave the cavern, and the Devil would seize the last one. That one would remain with him in hell.

The students were nervous because Midsummer's Day was coming. But when the day came, Axular said to them: I'll stay and go last myself.

The students began filing out. The Devil stood at the door and each student uttered the same sentence: "Grab who's behind me." And so it went, until Axular's turn arrived. The writer, too, said, "Grab who's behind me," and the Devil took Axular's shadow. He was left with no shadow his whole life long.

But having no shadow was extremely suspicious. It implied that when he died he would be going along to hell himself. For that very reason, in a number of other folktales it's told that Axular did get his shadow back at last, after passing one kind of test or another.

But the doubt did persist until not that long ago.

The priest and writer Jean Barbier put paid to all doubts. At the start of the twentieth century, because the cemetery at Sare needed renovating, they opened Axular's tomb. They saw that the writer's body was spotless, it had not decomposed. Barbier couldn't contain his joy. Beyond a doubt, Axular had managed at long last to get into heaven. Since they considered a body's staying whole and sound to be proof of holiness at that time.

The truth is different. The body was well preserved because the soil in Sare is clayey. But who could care less about that at this late date.

I began to think about Agirre. That gesture of not showing Azkue his house.

Our literary tradition bears a resemblance to Agirre's parents' house, small, poor, disorderly. But the worst thing is its being secret. We need to invite the people passing by to come into our house and offer them something there, even if that something is hardly anything.

We have the tradition we have and that's what we have to go on with; meanwhile, however, attracting as many people as possible to it. The best way to air out a house is to open up the windows.

Don't forget to make the time to tend the flowers too.

23

NEW YORK CITY

Fish and trees are alike. Loss makes our time specific. I spent a lot of time looking at Arteta's murals in the Bilbao Fine Arts Museum, thoughtful. Looking at one of the figures in the mural. It's far in the background. Behind the accordion player and to the right, a boy and two girls appear.

The boy goes first. He's making as if to strike the tambourine he holds. The middle girl is touching his back. That girl is being embraced by a girl behind her, whose chin nestles on her shoulder. I concentrate on the girl in the middle, she looks unnerved, gazes shyly straight at the viewer. She's the youngest of all the figures in the picture, no doubt about it.

I don't know if I should believe Mum or not, I don't know if this, too, might not be another apocryphal story, I don't know if Granddad Liborio was lying on that visit he made with Mum to this museum. The thing is, Granddad told our mother that that was Grandmother Ana, not to tell anyone, but he wanted to share that secret with her.

That right there is the only existing image of Grandmother Ana when she was young, young and happy. The photographs at home were taken a little later, the weariness showed in her eyes and her hair had begun going grey. But in the mural for

Bastida's house she can't be more than fourteen, she has her whole life in front of her.

Ana died young, she was no more than forty-five when she passed away. Liborio, fifty-two. When Liborio died there was an enormous rainstorm and a lot of boats that were moored in the river sank in the storm. Among them, Liborio's *Dos Amigos*. Cano, one of Grandmother Ana's brothers who lived in Bilbao, stayed in the house in Ondarroa for several days after Liborio's funeral. Cano was a mechanic by trade and he had the boat hoisted from the water, took out the motor and with the help of his grandson set it up in the living room at the house. There, he disassembled every piece of it, cleaned each one and reassembled the motor. Then, he called for a bit of fuel.

The motor of the *Dos Amigos* sparked to life in Liborio's house, full speed ahead, and it beat like an old heart in there.

"A poetical image truly, that motor business," the film director Vojtech Jasny said to me as we strolled along North Street, right by the place where my grandparents' house had been. Because I'd told him about the rebirth of the *Dos Amigos* as we stood right where the house had stood in its day. I first met Vojtech at that New York supper, the supper at Jose Fernandez de Albornoz and Scott Hightower's. In 1976, the San Sebastian Film Festival had given him their top award and he wanted to revisit these places he'd been through in his youth. One June day, because he wanted to get to know the Basque coast, we showed him around Ondarroa, along with a few other towns. In Ondarroa, we climbed to the Antigua hermitage, since the place is glorious and since from way up there a large stretch of the Basque coastline is visible, Biscay, Guipuzcoa and Labourd all at once.

When we reached the hermitage I told him the old stories and beliefs related to it, the ones Aunt Margarita and my grandparents told me when I was little. Among them I told him of the gifts of the Nazarene. How if you give a kiss with your hand to the glass over the image that stands in a corner of the hermitage it enlightens your mind. How it drives bad thoughts from the heart and lights up the imagination.

And half kidding, half not, I said that I, too, often came to ask for his help, especially when I have to start on a new book and have no ideas. And so, following the old usages of a former time, we both gave the image a kiss with our hand.

Once outside we went up in the bell tower. The view was wonderful from there. Because from up there you can see all the way to Donostia and Biarritz, and even La Rhune if there's good weather.

But Vojtech didn't look at the landscape for long. He stood watching the children who were playing in a pasture beneath the tower. In an instant he'd taken up that old camera of his and begun filming. The children who were playing there were two little girls. One of them black and the other white. Both of them born in the town. They were catching butterflies, with a sheet. They'd leap with the sheet and fall down. Then they looked inside the sheet to see if the butterfly was still in there.

The children don't catch any butterflies and, tired of the game, decide to head for home. Vojtech leaves off filming and calls thanks to the girls from up there. They pass below us, speaking in Basque.

I recall something that happened when I was little. While Franco was on his deathbed, there'd been some shootings not many days before and the police were going from house to house carrying out a general rummage everywhere. At our place, too, Mum gathered up all the papers that could be dangerous, leftist anti-Franco posters, reports, pamphlets, and caused them to disappear, as so many others were doing as well.

Soon enough Mum saw the *guardias'* black automobile in the street below. She watched them from the window. The *guardias* were zipping around here and there, as if they were lizards, like lightning. In a single bound they were at our door, ordering her to open up.

The head of the *guardias* entered the house very confidently, he had clear suspicions and was sure of finding a trace of something in that house. He ordered his *guardias* to ransack everything floor to ceiling, all drawers, all closets, the narrowest crack anything could be hidden in, to search it well.

One room remained to be examined. "It's my daughter's room," Mum warned them in Spanish. "She's sick." *Es el cuarto de la niña. Está enferma.* Though my sister was in bed they had no hesitation about rummaging around in that room as well.

All of a sudden, one of the *guardias* found something in a drawer beside my sister's bed and called to his chief. He came over quickly. Mum was suddenly terrified. And doubtstricken. Had she in fact got everything gathered up tidily. Had she forgotten some piece of paper. She was totally sunk. She looked at the child, pitifully.

"Don't worry, Mum, they're songs," my sister said, in Basque, in her thin sickly voice. *Lasai ama, kantak dira.* The head of the *guardias* became agitated. He asked what the child had said.

"She has a fever. She wants water," Mum blurted out in Spanish. *Tiene fiebre. Quiere agua.*

The *guardias* got the hell out of the house without finding anything.

The near-secret language of the time got my mother and sister though that fix in those dark years. They used the old language to protect themselves. Nowadays, in their turn, those two little girls who'd gone to catch butterflies were using the same language, but to play in. Even that one who was the daughter of people from Senegal.

Vojtech couldn't believe it. "This scene is wonderful!" he said to me, wide-eyed. "Even if I had all the money on earth I couldn't possibly shoot this, that naturally. Fiction is fiction and life itself is another thing entirely," he said, before taking up his camera and filming some more.

He came over to me and said, in English, "It works!" At first I didn't understand him. He meant the ritual of the Nazarene, that its virtues had worked, it had had its effect on him. He'd kissed the image with his hand and just moments later a miracle had occurred.

That had been the most beautiful scene he'd ever filmed. *"It works!"*

I wondered how many things I've asked the Nazarene for myself. How many times he's paid attention to me and how many he hasn't, believe it or not. Often I've asked him to help with Nerea and Unai, too many times even. For example, when I asked him to let Unai make a goal and they lost the game, that was pushing it.

Losing and winning. Death and birth. Most children are born into our world at age zero. But there are in fact some of them who are born a few months old, or three years

old, or seven. Unai was born right before my eyes at age
thirteen.

BIRTH

At thirteen, you were born before my eyes.
Just like that, all at once.
It was a weird birth, since you were born
as we were having a pizza for supper.
There'd been no pregnancy,
no walking the floor, no changing diapers.
I never took you to school
holding your hand on the first day.
I didn't teach you hopscotch
or hide-and-seek either.
I didn't go down to the beach with you
to see that dying dolphin.

I swear I'd long to have done all that,
I feel its absence every single day.
But you were born at age thirteen,
just like that, all at once, and over pizza.

I know for sure that you were truly born
in the cold spring of Denmark

and there was ground-frost on your birthday.
I know for sure that you do have a father,
you have people all over who love you,
friends, cousins, aunts, grandparents
and, obviously, a mother.
Of course, no one at all is only anyone's.
We have to learn to share the ones we love.
And I'm another, last to get in line.

Just to say,
I feel like a child myself when I am with you
and with you I buckle down and learn,
as if I knew nothing of hopscotch,
as if I were seeing dolphins for the first time.

Just to say,
your birth is real for me;
despite your being born at thirteen,
just like that, all at once, and over pizza.

After landing, images of the runway reappear on the plane's screen. The broken lines. Leaving the runways behind, the aircraft heads for the terminals, very slowly. "It's been a pleasure," Renata says to me and holds out her hand. She takes up her purse. The flight attendants are still seated, but even so people have started to turn on their phones. Renata gets a text message on hers. "Please, I need some help," the message says. The airplane has come to a stop at last. "Welcome to New York City."

Ondarroa, October 14, 2008.

ONDARROA: DEEP-SEA VESSELS

Achondo	Goizalde Eder
Akilla Mendi	Gran Boga Boga
Ama Lur	Hermanos Solabarrieta
Andra Maixa	Idurre
Antonia Carnero	Ituarte
Aralarko Mikel Deuna	Itxas Ondo
Arbelaitz	Itxas Oratz
Artabide	Jerusalén Argia
Arranondo	Jerusalén Argitasuna
Arretxinagako Mikel Deuna	Landaverde
Asmor	Larandagoitia
Beti Gure Javier	Larrauri Hermanos
Cibeles	Legorpe
Combarro	Leizarre
Chemaypa	Mañuko Ama
Dolores Cadrecha	Náutica
Goierri	Nuestra Señora de Bitarte
Goitia	Nueva Luz de Gascuña
Goizalde Argia	Nueva Luz del Cantábrico

Nuevo Tontorramendi

Ondarrutarra

Ormaza

Pattiuka

Pío Baroja

Plai Ederra

Río Itxas Ertz

San Eduardo

Saturán Zar

Sesermendi Barri

Siete Villas

Solabarrieta Anayak

Talay Mendi

Toki-Alai

Toki-Argia

Txanka

Txori Erreka

Urre Txindorra

ACKNOWLEDGMENTS

The excerpt from Italo Calvino's *Six Memos for the Next Millennium* on pages 62–63 is from Patrick Creagh's translation (Harvard University Press, 1988).

Lyrics on page 150 are from "Don't Know Why," performed by Norah Jones, written by Jesse Harris, from the album *Come Away with Me* (Blue Note Records, 2002).

The translation of "Birth" was first published in *Little Star* 3 (2012).

"The Gravestones in Käsmu" first appeared in English, in a slightly different version, in *Guernica*'s March 12, 2009, issue.

Coffee House Press began as a small letterpress operation in 1972 and has grown into an internationally renowned nonprofit publisher of literary fiction, essay, poetry, and other work that doesn't fit neatly into genre categories.

Coffee House is both a publisher and an arts organization. Through our *Books in Action* program and publications, we've become inter-disciplinary collaborators and incubators for new work and audience experiences. Our vision for the future is one where a publisher is a catalyst and connector.

LITERATURE
is not the same thing as
PUBLISHING

Funder Acknowledgments

Coffee House Press is an internationally renowned independent book publisher and arts nonprofit based in Minneapolis, MN; through its literary publications and *Books in Action* program, Coffee House acts as a catalyst and connector—between authors and readers, ideas and resources, creativity and community, inspiration and action.

Coffee House Press books are made possible through the generous support of grants and donations from corporations, state and federal grant programs, family foundations, and the many individuals who believe in the transformational power of literature. This activity is made possible by the voters of Minnesota through a Minnesota State Arts Board Operating Support grant, thanks to the legislative appropriation from the Arts and Cultural Heritage Fund. Coffee House also receives major operating support from the Amazon Literary Partnership, Jerome Foundation, McKnight Foundation, Target Foundation, and the National Endowment for the Arts (NEA). To find out more about how NEA grants impact individuals and communities, visit www.arts.gov.

Coffee House Press receives additional support from Bookmobile; Dorsey & Whitney LLP; Elmer L. & Eleanor J. Andersen Foundation; Fredrikson & Byron, P.A.; the Matching Grant Program Fund of the Minneapolis Foundation; Mr. Pancks' Fund in memory of Graham Kimpton; the Schwab Charitable Fund; and the U.S. Bank Foundation

The Publisher's Circle of Coffee House Press

Publisher's Circle members make significant contributions to Coffee House Press's annual giving campaign. Understanding that a strong financial base is necessary for the press to meet the challenges and opportunities that arise each year, this group plays a crucial part in the success of Coffee House's mission.

Recent Publisher's Circle members include many anonymous donors, Patricia A. Beithon, Anitra Budd, Andrew Brantingham, Dave & Kelli Cloutier, Mary Ebert & Paul Stembler, Jocelyn Hale & Glenn Miller, the Rehael Fund-Roger Hale/Nor Hall of the Minneapolis Foundation, Randy Hartten & Ron Lotz, Dylan Hicks & Nina Hale, William Hardacker, Kenneth & Susan Kahn, Stephen & Isabel Keating, the Kenneth Koch Literary Estate, Cinda Kornblum, Jennifer Kwon Dobbs & Stefan Liess, the Lambert Family Foundation, the Lenfestey Family Foundation, Sarah Lutman & Rob Rudolph, the Carol & Aaron Mack Charitable Fund of the Minneapolis Foundation, Gillian McCain, Malcolm S. McDermid & Katie Windle, Mary & Malcolm McDermid, Daniel N. Smith III & Maureen Millea Smith, Peter Nelson & Jennifer Swenson, Enrique & Jennifer Olivarez, Alan Polsky, Robin Preble, Jeffrey Sugerman & Sarah Schultz, Nan G. Swid, Grant Wood, and Margaret Wurtele.

For more information about the Publisher's Circle and other ways to support Coffee House Press books, authors, and activities, please visit www.coffeehousepress.org/pages/donate or contact us at info@coffeehousepress.org.

About the Spatial Species Series
Youmna Chlala and Ken Chen, series editors

The Spatial Species series investigates the ways we activate space through language. How do we observe where we are? How do we mark and name our behavior in space? How does a space occur as a midpoint between memory/history and future speculations? We pass over monuments, tourist spots, and public squares in favor of serendipity and détournement: non-spaces, edges, diasporic traces, and borders. Georges Perec revealed the value of how we relate to the infra-ordinaire. Such intimate journeying requires experiments in language and genre, moving travelogue, fiction, or memoir into something closer to eating, drinking, and dreaming.

Youmna Chlala is a writer and artist born in Beirut and based in New York. She is the author of the poetry collection *The Paper Camera.* She has published in *BOMB, Guernica, Aster(ix), Bespoke,* and *Prairie Schooner,* for which she won an O. Henry Award. Her artwork has been exhibited at the Bienal de São Paulo, Lofoten International Art Festival, and Performa Biennial, as well as the Hayward Gallery, the Drawing Center, Art in General, Art Dubai Projects, and Kunsthal Charlottenborg.

Ken Chen won the Yale Younger Poets Prize for his book *Juvenilia,* which was selected by Louise Glück. From 2008 to 2019 he served as the executive director of the Asian American Writers' Workshop. He is attempting to rescue his father from the underworld, a site that serves as an archive for all that has been destroyed by colonialism.

About the Translator

ELIZABETH MACKLIN is the author of the poetry collections *A Woman Kneeling in the Big City* and *You've Just Been Told.* A 1994 Guggenheim Fellow in Poetry, she received, in 1998, an Amy Lowell Poetry Travelling Scholarship, which allowed her to spend a year in the Basque Country, beginning studies in Euskara. Her translation of Kirmen Uribe's first poetry book, *Meanwhile Take My Hand,* was published in 2007. In addition to *Bilbao–New York–Bilbao,* she has translated numerous multimedia works in which Uribe has been involved. In the Basque Country she is a member of Zart Cultural Center.

Composition of *Bilbao—New York—Bilbao*
by Bookmobile Design & Digital Publisher Services.
Text is set in Spectral.